PRIDE UNLEASHED

CATHRYN FOX WRITING AS CAT KALEN

1

The night is thick, dark, and ominous—much like my current disposition. All around me the vineyard's nightlife falls mute, the cacophony of familiar sounds muffled beneath the heavy, menacing mood. Tension hovers overhead like a threatening rain cloud and my flesh tightens, waiting for the sky to crack open and fracture the silent night. Even the crickets stand down, their chorus hushed as they sit watching, waiting, listening for the hammer to fall, or in this case, the silver to pierce.

It unnerves me to think that the nocturnal creatures surrounding the estate—a mansion where I'd once been imprisoned—instinctively know that I, along with the pack of wolves at my back, are walking head first into danger and chances of survival are slim at best.

Not unless I can deceive him. The master. A coldblooded human who kept me under his strict control for seventeen long years. The same man who taught me to trick, to lure, to embrace my primal side in an effort to hunt the ruthless drug dealers who dared to cross him. But I'll have to put on my best performance yet if I want to fool the soulless predator who uses both silver and abuse to dominate his wolves.

And they call me the monster.

The second I surrender and he slaps a collar around my throat, I know what I'll have to do—convince him that I hadn't run away from the compound and had only been following his orders to hunt down a rogue wolf.

But showing no emotion in the face of an enemy who is as cunning as he is powerful might not be as easy as it once was. Not after everything I've been through. The fact that I've changed while running in Olympic National Park with the rogue wolf in question, however, is a point in my favor. The master no longer knows all my weaknesses.

Or any of my strengths.

I angle my head to see Logan, the boy/wolf who wound himself around my heart and helped me learn so much about the world, and about the girl inside me. When my eyes lock on his, my stomach punches into my throat and I swallow a cry of anguish.

Emotions crowd me because I realize Logan's fate is in my hands and I know what will happen to him once I turn him over to the master. I must abandon him like he's nothing more than a tick on my ruff, like what happened between us in that cave two weeks ago during the full moon was nothing more than a diversionary tactic. Despite our bond, I understand it's the only way we can get inside the fortified compound, the only option we have. But it still doesn't make feeding him to the wolves, so to speak, any easier.

I smile at my new mate but my expression slips when I turn away. The truth is I'm frightened. Frightened for Logan. Frightened for the pack of wolves at our backs, for the pack still trapped inside—what will happen if I can't get them out? And I'm frightened for Stone, the alpha who pretended to be my enemy but who risked his very life to save mine.

I can only hope that the boy I've known since childhood was able to use his wit and resourcefulness to stay alive. But what if I'm wrong? What if the master kills him because of me?

I draw in a sharp breath and work to desensitize. I can't let panic get the better of me. Not now. Not after I've come so far.

Keeping to the shadows and camouflaging ourselves in the hostile night, my footsteps slow as we reach the long winding driveway leading up to my former master's estate. With my sight unhindered by the darkness, I glance past the thick iron gate defending the perimeter and take in the sprawling mansion nestled at the foot of Mount Sirren.

On the south ridge of the mountain, overlooking the estate, fields of grapevines provide a gorgeous backdrop to the majestic manor. As I inhale the familiar scents, I struggle to tame the wolf pacing restlessly inside me, but I can't seem to marshal the unease seeping from my every pore.

Even though our aim is to get in and out as quickly as possible—no one wants to be inside the compound any longer than necessary—it's still a risky plan, dangerous, and the scars marring my body are a constant reminder that disobedience comes with a price. If I make one wrong move, one small mistake under the master's watchful eye, not even the capable alpha beside me or the pack of werewolves who make up our small army will be able to step in and stop him.

Something I long ago vowed to do.

My ears perk for sound, and I note that the propane-fired cannons, a device used to scare birds from the vineyard, are quiet tonight. But come tomorrow they'll blast again. At least they'd better blast, because my plan to get the others out alive hinges upon it.

Floodlights sweep the area, splashing monstrous shadows over the manicured lawns and towering marble sculptures. As

I take in the array of statues fringing the walkway I can't help but think they resemble an armed band of soldiers ready to defend the empire, prepared to kill all those who threaten their leader. I look beyond them, and in the distance I spot the front door with its ornate, silver doorknocker.

As I glare at it, my heart thunders and my blood pumps faster. The majestic entranceway might look welcoming to most, but I know it's not. I know the cruelties that await us on the other side. But instead of heeding common sense and running in the opposite direction, we're walking straight back in, simply because it's the only way I can follow through with the vow I once made to myself.

Logan moves closer, sensing my discomfort. Unwilling to give in to my fears, I breathe in his comforting scents, pulling them deep into my lungs. The heady bouquet of clean earth —a fragrance that reminds me of cool, summer days— mingles with the fresh aroma of pine needles. The aroma seeps under my skin and as it travels through my veins I suddenly can't help but wish I was facing the master alone. I hate the risk Logan is about to take. Hate that he's so sure of me that he's willing to put his life in my hands.

Aware of the security cameras panning the area, I take a tentative step closer to the intercom outside the gate. But fear for Logan's safety has my stomach rebelling as the bulging black button taunts me. I want to reach for it, but I can't seem to move, my mind and body no longer functioning on the same wavelength.

Logan curls his hand around my waist, and I jump at his touch. He slides me a look as those perceptive blue eyes of his slowly move over my face, a careful assessment that makes me uncomfortable.

His voice is low, reassuring and I try not to fidget when he whispers, "It's going to be okay, Pride."

I force a smile and my wolf bristles, but I no longer let her take comfort in his touch, or the warm strength of his body. Right now I need to draw on my anger, because it's that anger that's going to keep my wolf sharp and keep us alive.

"Pride," he says again in that soft tone that always gets to me, then he pauses to add depth to his words when he states, "We've all got your back. Nothing is going to go wrong."

"I know," I respond and study his family as I work to keep my voice from sounding uncertain. Although Logan is smart, strong and skilled, we're no longer playing in his territory. While his world might have dangerous black bears, birds of prey, and wild, feral animals, the king of my jungle is far more deadly.

And we'd be wise to remember that.

With life and death hanging in the balance, a dark shiver pulses in my blood. Ignoring the warning sign, I reach out and stab the security button. My mind takes that time to run through various scenarios. As I wonder how the master will receive us, knowing that the next few minutes will determine our fate, I pull a gun from my back pocket and aim it at Logan's head.

I turn to look at Logan's uncle, Malcolm, the powerful leader of the handpicked group of wolves who make up our motley crew. Since I know very little about each wolf, their strengths and weaknesses, I had zero input into who came and who stayed back to oversee their small Canadian community near the border.

But I do know that those who are with us now have risked their lives to help me free the others and for that I'll always be grateful.

Malcolm gives me a curt nod, bringing my attention back to the crisis at hand, and then his brown eyes take on a serious edge when he looks past my shoulders.

I don't need to turn to know what he's looking at. I can hear the gears grinding on the security camera as it slowly pivots my way. Returning Malcolm's signal with a stiff nod of my own, and summoning every ounce of courage I possess, I watch the team of eight retreat, losing themselves in the inky darkness surrounding the estate.

Once they've disappeared, I draw a fueling breath to clear my thoughts and remember what my father taught me when I was just a pup, before he blew out of my life like a leaf caught in an updraft. Never let them see your fear.

But thoughts of my father have my head spinning and fill me with a million questions. Mainly, could he still be alive?

I square my shoulder and begin to turn, to face the firing squad about to descend upon us, but moments before the camera lands on me, Logan's cousin, Gem steps from the darkness to give me a brisk hug.

"Grasshopper," she whispers into my ear. I instantly remember Logan once calling me grasshopper, but before I can ask what she means, she's gone, disappearing as quickly as she'd appeared, a bright shiny jewel dimmed by the ebony blackness owning the night.

I shift my focus to Logan and I'm about to question him. I want to ask what Gem means, but I also want to know why Malcolm would bring a spirited, energetic girl like her along— one who would surely collapse in the heat of battle. But he squeezes my arm in a silent message, letting me know it's time to focus.

A look passes between us, and then he lowers his head like a broken puppy—one who was just brutally kicked. My heart misses a beat as I watch him put on his game face and execute our plan to perfection. This strong yet gentle alpha never fails to amaze me and everything about him touches me in places I never knew existed until we met.

But I can't think about that right now, can't think about how he makes me feel so warm and secure when I'm with him. Right now I have to get my head in the game and focus on the task at hand, because once that gate opens we'll be anything but safe.

When I tear my gaze away from the boy who taught me how to trust, I remove all emotion from my face and look pointedly at the metal gate. Once again I remind myself that this risky plan needs to go down without a hitch, otherwise I might not ever feel Logan's warm touch again.

Shivers skitter down my spine at the sound of the oxidized hinges yawning open, yet I keep my face blank, my eyes vacant. Less than a split second later the sound of squealing tires reaches our ears. I brace myself for battle and blink against the glaring headlights aimed our way.

It appears the firing squad has arrived.

I peer into the darkened windows of the approaching vehicle and spot Lawrence, one of the handlers who takes pleasure in using a rough hand to restrain the wolves. I pan the inside of the vehicle and note that he's brought two body-guards as backup, the same ones I'd managed to ditch and elude at Olympic Park some three weeks ago.

The bulletproof SUV they're traveling in screeches to a halt just inside the gate. The three slowly emerge from the oversized luxury Blazer, and a crooked yet cautious smile curls Lawrence's thin lips as his dark, beady eyes lock on mine.

"Well, well," he says, as he swirls a metal collar around his index finger. It doesn't go unnoticed by me that he's using the thick, steel plated driver's side door to shield his body. That action speaks volumes and reminds me that while I'm the one they keep caged, he's the one who's truly afraid. "Would you look at what the cat dragged in?"

He exposes ugly stained teeth as his spiteful glance goes from me, to Logan, back to me again. I hold his gaze unflinchingly, fully aware of the two guns pointed at my head. I dart a quick look at the guards who are wielding those weapons, evil men who'd love to pump me full of silver should I make one wrong move.

As I take a moment to size them up my wolf stirs, but I calm her, warning her now is not the time to attack. She'll have her chance soon enough, I remind her.

Soon enough...

Lawrence clicks his tongue and makes a tsking sound as his focus settles on our bedraggled states. Logan's eyes inch up, but I shove my gun into his temple to stop him before he can challenge the handler. His head jerks and he growls deep and I can't quite tell whether he's simply playing along or if we're in real danger of him shifting and attacking.

As a protective wolf, and a boy who never goes down without a fight, I understand it's hard for Logan to let someone mistreat his mate, but the last thing I want him to do is defy the handler. It's much too soon for that.

"Nice and easy, kitty cat," Lawrence says and I hear the slight vibration in his voice when he crooks his finger. "Drop the gun and kick it my way."

I lower my weapon and let it fall to the pavement. It clangs on the ground, the sound puncturing the silence of the night. Using the inside of my foot I kick it toward him, giving a little more force than necessary. Despite having just warned Logan to behave, when it comes provoking Lawrence, I can't seem to help myself. Perhaps it's because of the hateful nicknames he calls me, or perhaps it's because he takes such pleasure in bullying the elders—older wolves who've been beaten and broken. Either way, antagonizing him is worth the wounds that come with disobedience.

The pistol skids past him, and I can feel the strain of Logan's eyes on me, a silent warning. But, just like old times, that little stunt earns me a scowl from the handler and the familiarity of it all helps me regain my focus and concentrate on my next move in this deadly game of cat and mouse.

The bodyguards watch the tense exchange between handler and wolf, and their heads bob back and forth like they're waiting for some sort of signal. Lawrence nods toward the gun and grits his teeth.

"Get it," he orders the man directly behind him, and when the burly guard bends to retrieve the weapon, Lawrence hurls the collar at me, much harder than necessary.

I know he's hoping to catch me off guard, but when I snatch it out of the air with practiced ease, his beady eyes narrow and his lips tighten in annoyance.

Glaring at me, he juts his chin toward Logan. "Leash him up, pet," he says evenly, not wanting me to know how much I've rattled him, but his words belie his emotions. I can smell his anger: hot, gurgling rage bubbling to the surface like a cauldron brimming with decomposing flesh.

The primal side of me howls at the putrid scent and my skin itches in response, my thin flesh burning like a thousand angry bee stings as my wolf cries to break free and go for Lawrence's throat.

Working diligently to fight off the change in the face of my enemy, I turn to Logan. My fingers brush along his neck as I snap the collar around his throat. When his gaze flickers to mine there is nothing I can do to ignore the sick feeling mushrooming in the pit of my gut.

This boy has come to mean so much to me—everything to me—and I can't stomach the thoughts of the abuse he's bound to endure at the hands of my brutal master. Our eyes meet and I can feel him reaching out to me, wrapping himself around my soul in a gesture meant to soothe, calm. Reassure.

"*No. Run!*" A hard, angry voice thunders inside my head, only I quickly realize it's not my voice frantically yelling at me to flee.

Caught by surprise I gasp out loud, my stomach cramping so hard I stagger forward. I clamp my hands over my ears to block the piercing noise, completely unprepared for the violent intrusion.

The sounds of guns cocking quickly pull me back and I struggle to compose myself. Dying now would simply interfere with my mission. And I refuse to let that happen. I take a deep fortifying breath, desperate not to blow our plan.

Knowing what I need to do to regain my focus, I think of my mother, my father, the elders, the puppies, and all the others who were killed or tortured by the master's hands. Anger erupts inside me and I use it to smother the confusion rattling my brain.

Unaware of the voice in my head, Lawrence challenges, "Are we going to do this the hard way or the easy way?"

As Lawrence's question hovers like a loaded bullet, the voice barks again, although this time it's louder and much more insistent. "*Run, Pride! It's not safe for you here.*"

Violent, chaotic images flash through my mind and I swallow the saliva coating my tongue, suddenly uncertain as alarm bells jangle, urging me to heed the warning.

"*Stone, don't!*" I bark back. "*It's okay,*" I hurry to explain. "*It's not what you think. I've come with a plan.*"

Feeling disoriented, I widen my stance and from my peripheral vision I catch the way Logan is watching me, his blue eyes darkening in distress as they lock on mine. That's when it occurs to me that he knows.

He knows Stone is in my head. Connecting with me in a way my own mate can't.

I shake the buzz from my brain to clear it and that's when I realize what this all means. Stone is alive! He hadn't been killed by the master because I ran away and he failed to bring me back. I'd spent the last couple weeks agonizing over his safety, knowing I couldn't bear it if anything happened to him because of me. I exhale a relieved breath and inside my wolf wails with joy at that small, unexpected surprise. Not only am

I ecstatic to learn that Stone is alive, we can use all the help we can get to pull off our risky plan.

As I focus in on Logan and take in the dark, troubled shadows beneath his eyes I can't help but feel an odd sense of betrayal for allowing another alpha into my thoughts. But it's not my fault that Stone and I defy nature and can mentally communicate when in human form. I realize it's not something the other wolves can do, and I can't explain why the two of us are an exception to the rule. All I know is that we are.

"Well," Lawrence probes as he tosses me another leash, the air between us crackling with volatile electricity as he waits for my answer. "Is it the hard way or the easy way, kitten?" he asks again.

With no choice but to block Stone from my thoughts so I can fully concentrate on this current crisis, I catch the collar with a hand that bears deep purple scars—whip wounds received from doing things the hard way. But lessons learned have taught me when to push and when to back off.

Without averting my gaze in a show of submission like I'm supposed to, I continue to glare at Lawrence. After all, the handler wouldn't expect anything less from me. The cold metal collar sends chills scurrying down my spine as I secure the restraint around my neck and snap it in place, my compliance answering his question.

When metal grinds metal, the lock sliding home, Lawrence visibly relaxes because he knows once I'm leashed, shifting is impossible. Not unless I want to put breaking my neck at the top of my to-do list. And right now those top spots are reserved for a select few.

Lawrence steps away from the vehicle and I can't help but bare my teeth as he hooks a heavy chain to my collar and gives it a good hard tug. I jerk forward, my neck nearly snapping like a dry twig, and I can feel Logan's tension spreading like an unleashed virus.

Before it infects Lawrence and causes him to react, I want to tell Logan to back down. We can't break cover, or let the handlers or anyone else in the compound know what we mean to each other. In this prison our feelings for one another will simply be used against us.

I slant my head to see my mate but no matter how hard I try I still can't speak to him telepathically when in human form. Using my eyes, I telegraph a message, and he correctly interprets the meaning. When he lowers his head in submission, I turn back to Lawrence and see the suspicion darkening his eyes.

"Should we get this over with?" I ask in an effort to take his focus off Logan.

There is a dangerous edge to Lawrence's voice, one I've never heard before when he focuses back in on me and says, "Over with? Oh no, Pride, this is far from over." The malicious look on his face tells me he knows something I don't and ribbons of fear trickle along the back of my neck when he adds, "For you, kitty cat, this is just the beginning."

2

I fight to steady the pulse thrumming in my throat as Lawrence punches a code into the number pad behind us. When the metal gate clangs shut, the loud sound resonates in my ears and I can't help but feel a certain amount of unease.

As the security system engages, the fence emits a low frequency hum, a warning that the power has been restored. And of course we all know what that means. Any attempt to scale the barrier will result in death. A familiar shudder moves through me when I steal a quick look at the key pad and strategize the best way to short-circuit the wires should our plan veer off course.

Once Lawrence has us both chained and under his control, he gives us a good hard tug to set us into motion. Purposely keeping two measured steps ahead of us, he ushers us up the long twisting driveway and I suddenly feel like cattle being led to the slaughter house.

Understanding the magnitude of our actions, and that we're about to walk into the lion's den, I gulp down my discomfort and deliberately keep my focus off Logan, unable to let my emotions get the best of me. Instead, I draw on my rage and glare at Lawrence as he hurries forward. While there is an air of bravado about the handler, I know he's afraid. But he isn't just afraid of me and what I can do to him.

He's also afraid of the master.

In the master's house, the handlers and staff have about as much freedom as the wolves do. The master's employees are made up of illegal immigrants, ones who either follow the master's command or risk deportation. I wonder briefly if Lawrence would take his freedom if offered. That thought raises another one. Many of the wolves have been broken, so who in the compound is truly my ally?

Who can I trust?

Behind us the vehicle is left abandoned, the steroid-induced guards tight on our heels. They're both breathing heavy and my wolf can't help but take pleasure in the sound of their hearts pumping hard, can't help but bask in the delicious scent of their warm blood as it rushes through their veins at breakneck speed. It makes her hungry, feral, and edgy and since it helps keep her on the top of her game I let her inhale the enticing aromas, let her pull them deep into her lungs so she can savor them later—when she just might have to feed off them for basic animal survival.

As our footfalls slice the quiet, I scan my surroundings and sort through the different smells clogging the air, all the while looking for signs of danger. For the millionth time since awakening, I carefully run through our dangerous plan and calculate the risks, the threats I accounted for and the ones I have no control over.

When we reach the front door, Lawrence punches in another code. After the lock inches open, he turns the knob, uses his shoulder to shove the door open and hauls us inside.

The second I enter the grand entranceway I widen my eyes and commit the foyer to memory. Instincts dictate that I look for any type of change, anything that could hinder my escape plan.

That's when I take note of the new security system. The one Stone warned me about when he met up with me in the national park.

Surprised at finding the little white box so easily, my pulse leaps, but I draw a calming breath to slow the blood sprinting through my veins. The last thing I want to do is show any sort of reaction and raise suspicion. But it does make me wonder why the master never bothered to conceal the monitor. Perhaps he has no fears that his wolves can break the code and escape. Then I remember what Stone told me. The security system wasn't installed to keep us in, but rather, to keep something or some*one* out.

Who or what could the master possibly be afraid of?

As I consider that longer, I wonder how Logan plays into all of this. The master was, after all, desperate to capture the rogue wolf alive. So desperate, in fact, that he risked sending out his best tracker when there was a high possibility that I'd run. Was the master worried that Logan could lead a team of wolves back if he made it to his pack in the Canadian mountains?

Or was he worried about something else entirely?

The hairs along my arm prickle and I turn back to face Lawrence, fully expecting him to lead both Logan and me into the east wing, to the master's office at the far end of the mansion. But when he separates us, handing Logan off to one of the guards, I try to appear unaffected by this surprise parting.

I watch Logan go, catching one last glimpse of him before he disappears from my line of vision. Once he's gone, I push down my anxiety and work to convince myself that this wolf —this teenage boy who's come to mean so much to me—can handle whatever punishment the master is about to inflict upon him. Because the alternative is much too difficult for me to consider.

Lawrence herds me past the small security office just inside the main entrance. I peruse the guard manning his station, then switch my focus to the vast array of monitors in time to catch fleeting images just beyond the perimeter. I narrow my focus, and my gut recoils when I realize something is out there.

Something, dark, sleek, and stealthy.

Something that looks cat-like, only bigger. My instincts go on high alert, every nerve ending in my body coming alive as my wolf clamors to take chase.

Acutely aware that my team is also out there while some unidentifiable danger lurks in the shadows, tendrils of unease slither restlessly through me. I blink my eyes and try to figure out who or what is prowling around the master's private kingdom. But before my brain can decipher what kind of creature is stalking the vineyard, I'm led toward the back stairwell.

That's when it occurs to me that Lawrence is taking me to my former cage in the bowels of the estate. My feet come to a resounding halt, troubled by this turn of events.

"I want to see the master," I say, eager to face him here and now, partly because I want to get the dreaded meeting over with and partly because I don't want to be tossed into my pen for the remainder of the night, wondering about Logan's fate. His future. The torture he's about to endure.

One dark eyebrow shoots up, mocking me. "Since when do you call the shots around here, pet?" He draws out the word pet just to taunt me. But I can't let that get to me right now. I have more important matters to deal with.

Like gaining my enemy's trust.

I need the master to believe my rehearsed lies otherwise he might keep me from the courtyard tomorrow. If I don't set my plan into motion at the proper time, there is a good chance I won't get another shot at this and my mission to free the others and demolish the master once and for all could be over before it even begins.

That thought has anger rising in my throat and a sick, nervous feeling rushes through my bloodstream. But as Lawrence pins me with a glare, I understand what the master is doing, understand that this is simply another form of punishment, a means to break his rebellious wolf.

I also understand I'm in no position to change it.

But I quickly remind myself that the night is young, and the master could still summon me. I need to cling to that crumb of hope because it's the only way I can face the next few hours of solitary confinement. I swallow down my apprehension and continue to let Lawrence lead me down the dimly lit hallway. We reach the cellar door and I wince when he flicks the light on.

I try to keep my breathing steady as I take in the cold cement floor at the foot of the stairs. The dank smell of the dirty cellar, wet and sticky against the inside of my nose, rises up to assault my senses and a guttural sound lodges in my throat.

After experiencing freedom in the mountains—freedom to climb the ice-capped peaks, to drink from the rivers, and to live off nature—equal measures of dread and discomfort career through my veins. The last thing I want to do is descend those steps, only to end up locked up in that same small, suffocating cage that imprisoned me for the last seventeen years.

The very place that haunts my memories.

Forcing myself to stay calm, I stand there for a moment, my wolf howling frantically inside me. While she is fearless in the face of danger, her instincts are telling her to run, to listen to Stone's warning. I place my hand over my stomach to hush her, to remind her that it's only a temporary situation and soon enough we will be free again.

After I placate her, she crouches nervously and I question myself. Who am I'm really trying to convince? Me or her?

"Move it."

Lawrence shoves me hard but I manage to brace myself on the door frame moments before I tumble head first down the stairwell. My lips curl back to expose sharp canines, and as my nails elongate, nature urges me to shift. To pounce.

To kill.

I draw in a sharp, calming breath, my body burning from the inside out, but I know better than to shift with my collar on. Using every ounce of strength I possess I gather my control before it snaps like a taut bow and settle for a low throaty growl meant to intimidate.

Ignoring the warning rumble reverberating off the walls around us, Lawrence says, "Normally I'd say ladies first." He pauses mid sentence to look over my small frame. I follow his gaze and note that over the past few weeks my body has filled out quite considerably. Now that I'm no longer starving, my skin sports a soft pink hue and my ribs don't protrude quite as much as they used to. Something, I'm sure, the master will quickly correct.

"Except you're anything but lady. Isn't that right, kitty cat?" he scoffs. As I glare at him he adds, "In fact you're nothing but a runt with the body of a twelve-year-old boy."

That comment might have stung a few weeks ago, and while there is no disputing the fact that I am and always will be the runt of the litter, Logan has taught me to use my size as a strength rather than a weakness. He also made me very aware of my female body in other ways. But I know it's that awareness that is going to make it difficult for me to pretend I'm the same Pride that left here three weeks ago.

Because I'm not.

The light dims as I descend the stairs slowly, wondering who or what is waiting for me at the bottom. I don't expect to see Jace or Clover, the elders I've bunked with my entire life. My heart clenches and I breathe deep to push down my emotions when I think about them, think about the sacrifices they made to free me.

When stair number five creaks I hear a waking moan a few feet away. My eyes adjust to the dark and that's when I see Sandy, a young fertile female, stirring in Clover's old cage.

Her big brown eyes widen in surprise when I approach, but beneath that gleam I catch a glimpse of something else, something that has my hackles rising. I watch her carefully, trying to determine if I can trust her or if she's been broken.

As I look for some small telltale sign that the master has turned her from a playful pup into a killer watchdog, Lawrence opens my cage and shoves me in. When my feet skid to a halt on the dusty cement, I spin around to face him. Instead of closing the cage behind me, he widens it even more, the hinges groaning like a wounded wolf. While I expect him to hastily retreat, to run back to the master like the obedient handler he is, he surprises me by holding his ground in the darkened shadows, glaring down at me.

Caution aside, I bare my teeth. "What?" I growl, unnerved by the way those beady eyes of his are moving over my body.

He extends one hand, palm up and smirks. "Your clothes."

My heart drops into my stomach as I turn my focus to the fashionably ripped jeans and snug t-shirt covering my body, clothes lent to me by Gem and worn by every ordinary teenage girl on the outside, something I've always longed to be. Had I really expected that I'd be allowed to keep them inside the compound?

"Now," he orders.

I'm smart enough to know that stripping me of my clothes is simply another way of stripping me of my dignity and it's also a reminder that we're allowed to own nothing in this prison.

That *we* are nothing.

Since the old Pride never would have balked at being naked in front of the others my hands go to my t-shirt. Wanting to get this over with as quickly as possible, I grip the hem and peel it from my chest. Then I rip my jeans from my hips.

As I push them down my legs and kick them off, my skin crawls like a million insects nipping at my bare body. I scratch at my flesh and ignore the urge to grab a blanket to cover myself. Instead, I glare back and don't even bother to keep the disgust from my voice when I ask, "So I guess you have a thing for twelve-year-old boys then?"

Black eyes shoot daggers as his head comes up with a start, his fiery gaze scalding me with the power of a thousand burning suns.

"What are you talking about?" he spits back, practically frothing at the mouth as he pulls a vile face and glares at me in challenge.

I don't answer. I don't need to. He knows full well what I'm talking about. Before he can retaliate, the sound of Sandy shifting restlessly beside us gains our concentration and cuts the rising tension. In one swift move, Lawrence grabs my clothes off the floor, slams my door shut and smashes his hand down over my lock. The sound echoes in the room but I refuse to cringe as I hear the bolt slide home, refuse to give Lawrence that kind of pleasure.

But my wolf, knowing she is trapped inside this impenetrable prison for the entire night, wails in sheer agony and I can feel her spirit die just a little. The only time she ever felt alive was when she was running, when she was with Logan. I hush her, promising she'll have those things again, no matter what it takes.

"Don't let the bed bugs bite," Lawrence says, and I can hear his smug satisfaction as his lips twist in triumph.

I want to respond, want to let him know that while he won this battle I plan to win the war, but the words sit on the back of my tongue because I know when enough is enough. I grip the bars and glare at Lawrence's retreating back as he ascends the stairs and douses the lights, leaving us in complete darkness.

Once he's gone, I let loose a breath and step back. Shaking off my anger, I turn around and take in my old cot and ratty blanket, neatly draped over the worn mattress. At the end of my bed I find my white nightgown. Surprised, I pick it up and when the fresh scent of laundered clothing reaches my nostrils, I pull the gown to my nose and inhale. I can only assume Mica washed and folded it for me, but it does make me wonder if the aging housekeeper knew I'd return, either on my own, or by force. Then again, maybe she hadn't done it for me at all. Maybe they all believed I was gone for good and it's now time for one of the pups to move into my cage.

Only those who've reached puberty are allowed to have their own dens. Then they're put through a series of tests and agility training to determine who is the strongest—which two wolves will produce the finest offspring.

We have many elders who are well past their prime and are no longer reproducing, but they're kept alive because they're still great trackers. Right now, however, only Stone, Sandy and I are of breeding age—and that's one of the main reasons why I ran away three weeks ago.

After the master decided that I was good breeding stock, I knew I had to flee. Not only did I think Stone was my enemy, the last thing I wanted to do was bring puppies into this world to suffer at the hands of the master.

Thinking about Stone has me dropping my mental mind shields. I search for him, anxious to open communication again, to fill him in on our plan, but with the thick basement walls forming an impenetrable barrier, I can't quite tap into his thoughts.

After risking his life to give me my freedom, I know he's angry that I've come sauntering back into the compound like nothing happened between us at Olympic National Park. And if there is one thing I know, Stone's anger means trouble. I also know exactly who he'll direct that anger at. But surely he knows me well enough to understand that I'm not about to take my freedom at the expense of his or anyone else's.

I listen for sound upstairs, hoping the master is going to call for me as I pull my nightgown on over my chilled body and drop down onto my bed. Scurrying backward until my back is pressed against the cool cellar wall, I pull my knees to my chest and let the cement foundation suck the heat from my bones. The last thing I want to do is get too comfortable in this prison.

As my wolf growls softly, I turn my head to see Sandy. Curled into the fetal position, her long wheat-colored hair falls forward to mask her features. As I study her it suddenly occurs to me that's she's pretending to be asleep. But from the rise and fall of her chest I can tell she's wide awake and paying very close attention to her surroundings.

I struggle to figure out what's going on. Why did she go from surprised to cold when she first saw me coming down the stairs? Could it be because she's angry with me? Angry that the elders were killed because of me?

Sadness overwhelms me and I take a deep breath to drag the heavy air into my lungs. As I do I catch faded smells of Jace and Clover, but as I move past those scents, I catch another aroma. It's faint, but it's there just the same.

I pull it in, trying to decode it, trying to figure out why it's vaguely familiar to me. But the answer continues to linger just out of my reach. I wrack my brain until the ugly truth hits me harder than a blow to the gut. My heart goes into my throat and I jackknife from the cot.

"No!" I cry out, my glance moving to Sandy's belly, to determine how far along she is.

My fists pound on the metal bars, then I grip them until my knuckles turn white. Guilt eats at me for leaving her, for not being here to protect her from this kind of abuse. It should have been me the master bred, not her. She's too young. Too innocent.

I want to call out to her, to tell her how sorry I am. But when I see her lips curve like she's happy about her little secret another thought hits.

Who's the father?

Before I can consider it further, a loud noise at the top of the stairwell gains my attention. My eyes dart to my door, and my heart hammers against my chest when I hear angry voices followed by pounding footsteps and slamming doors. The master's dark, dangerous tone curls around me and squeezes my chest like a tight fist.

As air evacuates my lungs, every instinct I possess tells me I should have listened to Stone, because everything in the master's rage warns me that I'm in very serious trouble here.

Equal measures of fear and fury shoot through me, and my wolf—sensing that her life is in grave danger—growls in retaliation and prepares for a fight. My canines punch through my gums and I drop to the floor and hunker low, bracing myself as I wait for the ambush.

Honestly, I didn't think my first night back was going to be a pleasant one, but I didn't think it was going be my last one either.

3

Time slows to an agonizing crawl as I continue to wait. Seconds tick by and soon minutes turn into hours. I stay crouched low, hunkered down on my hands and feet, but when the invasion never comes I begin to suspect that the anticipation of an attack is far worse than any torture the master could possibly inflict upon me.

Perhaps that was his intention all along.

A long time later a noise finally penetrates the quiet of the cellar, and when I catch the tantalizing taste of bacon on the tip of my tongue I know morning is upon us.

Desperate to face the master, desperate to know what happened between him and Logan last night and what he really wants from my mate, I shake the fog from my sleep-deprived brain and prepare myself. My knees ache in protest as I pull myself to a standing position and stretch out my stiff limbs.

The sound of my popping joints echo in the quiet and my ears perk for sound from above. As I diligently wait for the upstairs door to creak open, fresh outside air rushes into my cell from the ventilation system and I drag the vineyard's scents into my lungs. Beyond the grapes I catch hints of rain in the air, and off in the distance I can hear the low, menacing growl of thunder.

Since it rarely rains in California, especially this time of year, I can't help but think the approaching storm is a warning sign of things to come. But with an autumn storm comes rain, and the downpour will help mask both the scent and the tracks of the wolves waiting in the shadows.

When I think about my small army, my mind briefly flashes back to those dark, vague images I glimpsed on the security monitors last evening. I can only hope that every-thing on the outside is going according to plan and my team is ready and awaiting the signal. If not, if by some chance there is a fatal flaw in our plot to overthrow the master it could mean...

Refusing to contemplate the prospect, I will the basement door to open and wait for a hint of morning light to filter downward. I can sense Sandy staring at me, sense the anger simmering just below the surface. When a low, threatening growl rumbles in the depths of her throat, a sinking sensation begins in my core and spreads onward and outward.

I slant my head to see the young wolf. With her golden hair hanging in wild curls, her cold, calculating eyes look stark against her small face and sunken cheeks. When those big orbs shoot silver darts into my back I feel nausea well up inside me.

Without bothering to hide her hate, she climbs to her feet and stalks to her door to await the handler. She wraps bony fingers around the bars and when I see how thin she's become, it renews my purpose to get her out of here, to get her safe, warm and properly fed.

Both sadness and guilt force my watery gaze back to the stairwell. While I'm unable to face those accusing eyes of hers, it doesn't mean I don't want to go to her, to pull her into my arms and console her. To let her know I hadn't abandoned her here while I chased game and gorged on fresh meat in Olympic National park.

I want to tell her how sorry I am about the elders and that I'll do whatever it takes to free her, to get her out from beneath the master's brutal control. But before I can push any of those words past the lump lodged in my throat, she speaks first, and her words chill me more than a wintery dip in the icy cold ocean.

"He doesn't need you any more, Pride." Her tone is low, her voice laced with venom.

As I digest the meaning of her words, my blood pressure soars and my vision pulses, the room fading in and out of existence. Shock keeps me motionless and my body stiffens, my addled brain hardly able to digest and comprehend what she's saying to me.

When I hear a rustling sound I don't need to turn to know she's rubbing her belly, and I can hear the sheer pleasure in her young, naïve voice when she adds, "You're not the only one who can give him what he wants, you know."

As her words echo desperately in my head, I think about last night and comprehension slowly sinks in. It suddenly becomes perfectly clear to me that Sandy hadn't gone from surprised to cold because she's angry with me. She'd turned on me for one reason and one reason only. She wants the master to herself. Her wolf is threatened by mine—the only other fertile female in the compound.

When that reality registers, I want to scream at her. I want to cry for her. I want to break free of my cell and tear the master's head clear off his shoulders for what he did to her.

Tears prick my eyes and I swallow, hating that she's been broken, hating that she had to endure such torture at the hands of our cruel master. I can only hope that once I get her out from under his hold, I can help her heal and become whole again.

"You should have stayed away, Pride. You're nothing but trouble for the rest of us and no one wants you here."

Anger and sadness churn inside my belly as I briefly close my eyes against the flood of emotion. "Sandy—" I begin, not exactly sure what to say, but my words dissolve when my gaze shifts to her stomach.

Her eyes sparkle, her lips twist viciously. "You're nothing but a runt, Pride, and you could never have given a powerful alpha like Stone the offspring he deserved anyway."

Stone!

Unnerved by that wild implication my stomach sours and a bitter cold shudder runs along my spine.

Could it be true?

Had Stone done this to her?

The sheer lunacy of that notion has my legs going weak and my brain racing to catch up. Then again, what if he had no choice in the matter? The master isn't a man who tolerates mistakes or insubordination. What if mating with Sandy was the only way for Stone to prove his loyalties to the master after returning to the compound empty-handed?

I swallow. Hard. What would the master do to make me prove my loyalties?

As I think about Logan, my heart goes on a roller coaster ride. He's strong, I remind myself. The strongest wolf I know, physically and mentally. And while he's assured me numerous times that he can handle whatever punishment the master is capable of delivering, I can't help but worry. If you find a person's weaknesses, then you've found a way to destroy them, and if there is one thing I know it's that everyone has their breaking point. And it's only a matter of time before the master finds it.

For a minute I wonder about my own breaking point.

What would it take for me to back down, to become the obedient wolf the master wants?

When Sandy begins to hum a lullaby, one I'm familiar with from my days in the nursery, I get the distinct impression that she's trying to taunt me. Once again I wonder if Stone is the father, and what other corrupt things the master made him to do prove himself trustworthy.

That thought has my rage surging, and a volatile storm begins to brew inside me just as the door at the top of the stairs flings open. When light filters down, hot panic invades my stomach. I might have waited all night for a handler to come for me, to lead me to the master, but after learning Stone could be the father to Sandy's pups, the timing couldn't have been worse.

With my world tilting on its axis, I need a moment to compose myself, to desensitize, to concentrate on my mission. I look around frantically and when I spot my mother's old den it helps me remember my purpose, my commitment to destroy the master and make him pay for what he's done to us.

With no choice but to force Sandy's disturbing news to the back of my mind, I call on calm, and diligently struggle to get my head on straight. I'll need all my wits about me when I face the master and the last thing I want him to know is how desperate I am to get into the courtyard before noon.

I'm almost relieved when I see that it's Mario coming to let the dogs out. Mario has always been nice to me, but I can't ever forget he's one of them.

He stares at me longer than what's comfortable and I see the strain in his eyes, a new weariness that wasn't there three weeks ago. Holding his gaze I stare back, fully aware that Sandy is watching us with dark suspicion. I can only chalk her distrust up to her current condition, and that's she's been beaten and broken by a man who I'm going to enjoy destroying.

"Welcome back, Pride," Mario greets and while his voice isn't soft, it isn't hard either. His focus goes from me to Sandy, back to me again. He studies me carefully, like he's deliberating his next words. "Are you prepared for today's obstacles?" he finally asks but I can tell he wants to say something else as his tense glance flickers from me to the padlock dangling on the outside of my cell.

When the upstairs light glints on the shiny metal key, it occurs to me that the bolt is new. I'm not sure why that's important. But some part of my brain registers that it is. I store that information away for later as Mario inserts the key into the lock, but his hand slows before he twists it. I can tell he's waiting for my response, some kind of sign that I understand what he's saying.

Instead of responding I take a second to digest his cryptic words. As they settle in my brain I get the distinct impression that he's trying to warm me about something. Something that has nothing to do with the obstacle course we're forced to compete on every day and everything to do with the master.

Apprehension curls through me and once again my hackles bristle, my fearless wolf ready and anxious to face whatever danger lies ahead. As I acknowledge the strange new energy inside the mansion, I take a moment to wonder about the compound and all its secrets.

What's happened here since I've been gone?

As I peruse Mario it occurs to me he's being extra cautious around Sandy. It's clear that he knows she's been broken. But does he know I'm not? Is it possible that the handler can be trusted? When I go for his throat to overpower him will he shoot to kill, or will he back away and let me take my freedom?

He grabs my chain and I follow him out of the cage. I pad softly behind him, the cement so cold on the soles of my feet they begin to ache. Once he has Sandy leashed, he guides us up the stairs, and this time I fully expect him to take me to the master. When we reach the top, the cannon thunders outside the window and I take a moment to count the seconds between detonations. I checked the timing when I was outside scouting the estate, but it doesn't hurt to check again, just to be one hundred percent sure that the schedule hasn't changed since my escape.

My stomach grumbles but I ignore the warm, enticing scents of bacon, eggs, sausage and my favorite, hazelnut flavored coffee, as they fill the mansion. Mario leads us into the kitchen, toward the back courtyard, and when it becomes clear that he's actually taking me outside, instead of straight to the master's office, I try to keep the surprise from my face.

Since putting our plan together weeks ago I've done nothing but fret over my initial meeting with the man I hate, fully expecting a brutal, if not bloody, interrogation. Armed with a solid, believable story, I was prepared to spill lies, knowing I'd have to convince him of my loyalties before he'd let me out to mingle with the others.

I almost breathe a sigh of relief as I move toward the back door. Almost. Because everything in my gut tells me it can't be this easy.

Nothing in the compound is ever this easy.

Mica's indrawn breath reaches my ears when she sees me. Then she exhales sharply, reacting like she received a physical blow when she catches Sandy's dark, feral gaze. She quickly turns away and pretends to fuss with a stubborn loaf of bread.

The housekeeper has always been nice to me too, giving me extra scraps of food when no one is looking. But I don't acknowledge her this morning. Especially since the master's little watchdog is walking right beside me, studying my every move with entirely too much interest.

Using the clock on the stove, I do a quick check of the time and realize it's late morning as I'm led outside. The hairs along my neck tingle in anticipation because high noon will be here before I know it, and I must ensure everything is in place prior to that.

When I step onto the dewy grass, the heavy, sultry air dampens my flesh and beads of perspiration speckle my skin, now tanned from my week running along the mountain peaks. As my thin nightgown clings to my moist body, I tilt my head skyward. I note the four impenetrable stone walls surrounding us as I observe the dark clouds moving in from the north.

A storm is coming.

An odd shiver moves through me, but the sound of a starter gun pulls my focus and I jerk my head to the left in time to see two male wolves take to the obstacle course, both eager to win the race so they won't have to dine on scraps tonight.

Mario removes the collar from around my neck. "Get yourself ready," he says, then turns his attention to Sandy.

I take that time to gather my bearings and scan the courtyard, keeping my face blank as I anxiously search for Logan and pray that he's okay. But when my search turns up empty and I realize just how jam-packed the yard is, my senses go on high alert. I carefully study the herd of strangers, their faces and scents unrecognizable to me.

After a quick tally I estimate there to be at least twenty new shifters in the crowd. As I watch them, and note the probing way they're all looking back at me, intuitive intelligence warns me that the master is building himself an army. And a very powerful one, at that.

Realizing a compound full of newcomers isn't something I

had accounted for, something that could very well hinder my plan, panic bursts inside me. Desperate to find Stone, I look through the throngs of wolves, who are all in various stages of shifting. Not only do I need Stone's help, I want answers. Where did all these werewolves come from, and why does the master need them?

All around me deep guttural howls mingle with quiet conversation and as the noise ebbs and flows through the heavy air I lift my chin to take in the six trigger happy guards manning the grounds from their stony perch high above us.

As I study them, someone nudges me from behind. I spin, but receive a blow to the shoulder that has me whirling back around. Air rushes from my lungs with an oomph and my teeth clench hard. Before I can regain my balance, a bump to my left hip causes me to stumble. Twigs gnarl between my toes and pain zings up my leg. Fearing I'm about to hit the ground with an undignified thud, I widen my stance and let my nails elongate.

My wolf prepares to attack, anger boiling deep and heavy in her belly. But before she can shift into her primal form and challenge whoever is crowding her, a fistful of dirt is thrown into my face. I howl, and as the sound of my nightgown ripping mingles with my dark yowl it becomes glaringly apparent that I'm under attack.

Had the master orchestrated this punishment?

Is this what Mario had been trying to warn me about?

My wolf wails, eager to attack her assailants face on, to tear fur from bone and fill her mouth with warm, sweet plasma, but the click of the guns cocking above our heads has the mangy crew backing down. As they disperse, anxiety bombards me because I realize that this display of animosity toward me means these new wolves are loyal to the master. This could very well cripple my plan.

My mind races, trying to sort things through. Even if my

small army is able to take out the six armed guards when the cannon sounds at midday, how will I ever convince these broken wolves that I can offer them freedom? Will they allow me to lead them from the compound, or will they protect their master at all cost and turn on me?

As I eye the shifters with uncertainty, I press my hand to my stomach to settle my agitated wolf, but as I leash her, I know she has every right to be upset. This unexpected turn of events could mean the end of her freedom—and everyone else's.

Fearing the worst, I blink hard to squeeze the dirt from my eyes, desperate to clear my vision. I need to find Stone and I need to find him now.

"You shouldn't have come back."

As if my thoughts had somehow conjured him, I feel Stone closing the distance between us. I also feel the hot, seething anger emanating from his every pore.

Keeping my back to him as I gather my composure I answer with, *"How could I not?"*

His rage overwhelms me as he comes closer but the softness in his knuckles as they brush along my arm speaks of a deeper emotion, one he can no longer keep hidden from me. With my gut clenching, I spin around and I'm about to explain why I'm back, about to regurgitate my rehearsed speech in order to make him understand, but my lungs seize when I see the ugly purple scars marring his upper body.

Recent scars.

Scars inflicted by our master.

I bite the inside of my cheek hard enough to draw blood and when my fingers twitch, wanting in the most desperate way to soothe his sores—lashes delivered because of my disobedience—it forces me to fist my hands and anchor them to my sides.

I know better than to show emotion in this prison. For both our sakes.

"*This is my fault,*" I say quietly, barely able to keep my wolf contained as rage spikes my blood pressure.

My eyes go to Stone's and while I expect to see reproach in his dark gaze, what I see instead has my throat constricting and my heart aching for him.

His long, mussed hair brushes along his chiseled cheeks as he dips his head to better see me. The hardness on his face softens when he says, "*It's not your fault, Pride.*"

I gulp the heavy air but can barely fill my lungs as I scrutinize him. With my mind going in a million different directions, I assess both the physical and emotional damage done to his body and mind, and while I know he's lying, trying to protect me from the harsh truth, it does make me think of Sandy and what she said to me.

"*You're nothing but trouble for the rest of us and no one wants you here.*"

As Sandy's words echo in my head I want to tell Stone I'm sorry. For not believing in him. For not trusting him. For...*everything.*

But since I know nothing about forgiveness how can I expect him to simply put the past behind us.

"*Stone, I'm...I'm...*" I try to formulate the right words in my mind when I suddenly notice that the yard has grown exceptionally quiet. Even though we're speaking telepathically, and trying not to draw attention, many wolves are focusing on us with dark curiosity, and that doesn't bode well for either of us.

I glance back at Stone. His troubled eyes collide with mine and inside my head his voice is a soft, coarse rasp, one filled with raw emotion. "*Pride-*"

Despite the warmth of the day, a chill runs through me because I know he's thinking about that night in the cave, the night I gave myself to another. That has my thoughts careening to my new mate and worry for his safety gnaws at my insides.

What could the master want from him?

As I mull that worry over, one large raindrop lands on my forehead. An ominous cloud moves in overhead, darkening the courtyard. A cool breeze comes out of nowhere and rushes across my face, the whispering hush of danger following in its wake.

Stone's dark eyes are somber and I see a sadness that he can't hide as his gaze moves over my face. My throat clenches painfully and when I think about everything he's done for me I can't help but feel a sense of disloyalty to him.

For a moment we stand there in strained silence, then before I break down and cry at the unmasked grief clouding his face, I slice the tension by saying, "*I had to come back.*"

His mouth tightens. "*No you didn't.*"

"*Stone—*" I begin but he cuts me off.

He casts his eyes down and his look is intense when he begins, "*You need to listen to me.*"

"*No, you need to listen to me,*" I say almost frantic. "*We need to put a stop to this. You know it as well as I do.*"

His gaze darts nervously around the courtyard and I can tell he's uncomfortable but working hard to hide it. His jaw seesaws from side to side as he clenches hard. "*I told you, it's not safe for you here. Not now.*"

Every muscle in my body stiffens and the nerves tracking along my spine tingle. I look at him, my eyes searching his for answers. "*What's going on here? What is it you're not telling me?*"

Before he can speak, Mario steps up to us and directs Stone to the obstacle course. While I'm desperate for answers, desperate to put my plan into motion, I have no choice but to step away. I can't cause a commotion. It's too soon for that.

Anxiety flutters in my belly as I watch Stone take his place at the start line. I back out of the crowd and move to the sidelines, to lose myself in the shadows while I continue to count the minutes which suddenly seem to be ticking by far too quickly.

As I keep one eye on Stone, noting the way he negotiates the course with practiced ease, I press my back to the fortress wall and try to see inside the mansion, try to catch some sign that Logan is nearby, unharmed, ready and waiting for the signal.

I work to tamp down my nervousness while I focus back in on Stone's large, streamlined frame as he run through the course. But when he slows on the zig zags, worry fills me. It occurs to me how much time we're losing. Time we can't afford to lose.

Behind the clouds I know the sun is rising higher and higher in the sky and I know I have to have everything in place before it's directly overhead.

Stone finally finishes the course, and when he comes out the winner, he shifts back to human and pulls on his jeans. Then he turns to face me. From across the courtyard we stare at one another in mute silence and an excruciating looks passes between us.

The wind hums around the yard blowing dirt and debris across our faces and before I get a chance to tell him about my small army outside and what they're about to do, he weaves his way through the crowd and closes the distance between us. His face is serious, his eyes grave as he looks past my shoulders.

"*Not everyone wants or can be saved, Pride,*" he announces like he's already privy to my plan.

"*You're wrong,*" I say and give a hard shake of my head, refusing to believe him. If I did, that would mean I'd dragged

Logan and his entire family into my dark, dangerous world and put their very lives at risk for nothing.

When he gestures with a nod, I use slow careful movements and twist on the balls of my feet. Following his gaze I search through the throngs of wolves until I spot Sandy smoothing her hair off her face. She glares at me then shifts her stance to looks at Stone. When I watch her turn on her puppy charm in the face of the compound's alpha, I take note of the new scars decorating her flesh. The sight has my wolf howling and all I want to do is weep for her.

My eyes flick back to Stone's. "*She's-*" I stop, unable to bring the words to life, unable to give them meaning.

He gives a tight nod and his nostrils flare wide as he slides me a knowing look. "*Yeah, I know.*"

I lower my head and frown. "*Of course you do.*"

"*What's that supposed to mean?*"

The tension in his tone has my head jerking back up with a start. "*Nothing.*" I swallow, not at all sure how it makes me feel to know that Stone will soon have pups with Sandy. But I do know that the unwise sting of jealousy I'm experiencing makes me uncomfortable, especially since I've given myself to another—a powerful, caring wolf who is going against his own best interests to help me.

"*She wants out of here,*" I say more to convince myself than anything else. "*She just doesn't know it yet.*"

"*Are you sure about that?*" he challenges.

"*Yes,*" I snap, although I'm not sure about anything. Not anymore. Needing to redirect the conversation I rush out, "*We've come with a plan, Stone.*"

His dark eyes are explosive as they move around the courtyard and I know exactly who he's looking for and exactly what he'll try to do when he finds him. "*We?*"

"*Yes, we,*" I say, as I listen to the cannon boom in the distance.

I scan the courtyard and once again notice how much attention we've drawn. But despite the warning glares aimed my way, I realize it's too late to turn back now. I can't let doubt cloud my mission and I have to cling to the belief that once we take down the master, it will break the spell he has over these broken and abused wolves.

Knowing we need to move fast and get close to the handlers before my team on the outside attacks, I step closer to Stone and try not to appear conspiratorial when I say, "*I need you to pay careful attention to what I'm about to tell you, because we're all going to get out of here today and we need your help.*" I continue to speak, but stop short when I realize he's no longer listening to me.

I watch his eyes narrow unnaturally, and note the way he's sniffing the air. When he looks at a distant spot near the master's private entrance, the hairs on my nape prickle and tendrils of unease crawl over my skin like an army of red hot fire ants.

Stone gives a slow shake of his head, and the worry in his voice scares me when he says, "*Pride, oh hell, Pride, what have you done?*"

I spin around in time to see the master, shielding himself from the impending rainstorm with a black umbrella, but it's who he's with that sends my heart into overdrive and has cold flooding my veins.

Darkness churns inside my stomach as the master moves with purpose, each menacing step meant to intimate, to force me to react. As he baits me, his cold shrewd eyes search my face and it takes every ounce of control I have to keep my wolf from rushing at him when all I want to do is let her off her leash.

I look right at him, taking in the hard lines of his profile, then sever his lecherous gaze as I shift my concentration to the young girl anchored to his side.

Expression stricken, the girl lifts her lashes, and when her terrified green eyes flicker over mine, it occurs with dawning horror that the master has captured none other than Logan's cousin, the sweet and innocent Gem.

With her hands and feet in manacles, she shuffles alongside the master. I hiss when I watch her stumble, a riot of emotions overcoming me, congesting my ability to think with any sort of clarity.

As I stare at them from across the courtyard, I can taste Gem's tension like it's my own. It leaves a bitter residue on the back of my tongue and has sour bile punching into my throat.

I fight for a measure of control as I look her over, my brain registering the bright red scars on her forehead as well as the swollen puffy flesh around her blood crusted mouth. A chill scurries up my spine and air leaves my lungs in a whoosh when I realize just how badly this could turn out. Because the truth is, Gem, who has never known abuse in her entire life, and who has never, ever been confined by a cruel master, is in way over her head.

We all are.

My breath comes quicker, my pulse pounding in my throat as I clench and unclench my hands, berating myself for not calculating this risk. How will I ever get her out from his control before the cannon strikes at noon?

Thunder rumbles in the dark sky and when the clouds split open, the cold rain does little to soothe the hot rage rising inside me. Fat raindrops cake the dirt on Gem's torn clothes and dilute the blood dribbling down her trembling chin. The intoxicating scent gains the awareness of the restless wolves milling about and they begin to circle like the ravenous predators they've become since capture—since the master turned them into his puppets.

Guided by instinct, I make a move to go to her, but

Stone's hand comes down on my shoulder to stop me and the sheer strength of his grip doesn't go unnoticed. His fingers bite into my flesh, pinning me in place and when the word, "Don't," rumbles in the air, my footsteps still.

Before I can even think about my next move, the cannon sounds in the distance and my brain registers that it's high noon. I spin around frantically, my eyes surfing over the crowd, excepting to find a courtyard in chaos as my team closes in from the outside.

Except what I find instead has my heart hammering and my pulse racing like mad.

Panicked, my glance darts to the guards and dread floods my lungs, making it difficult to breathe when I find all six of them still standing tall, their guns directed at the courtyard as they police us dogs from above.

Apprehension surges through my bloodstream and I feel like my world is closing in on me. The impenetrable fortress walls seem to be inching closer and closer, squeezing the air from the yard and my arteries until I can barely comprehend how quickly things have fallen apart. I force myself to breathe slowly, my mind racing with unanswered questions.

What happened to my pack?

Our plan?

Thunder claps loudly snapping me back to reality, and as lightening streaks across the cloud bloated sky my nerve endings crackle in warning, my brain repeatedly screeching that this was not supposed to happen!

This was not supposed to happen!

With the world around me collapsing, everything inside me screams in alarm, my senses, emotions and thoughts running circles in my brain until my mind shuts down and my animal impulses come out full force.

Fearing the worst—a failed mission and a lifetime of captivity for all—there is nothing I can do to keep my primal side at bay. Fully understanding that something has been unleashed inside me, and that I won't be able to stop my caged wolf from turning mutinous, I deliver a yelp.

My torn nightgown rips clear of my body as I embrace the wild animal clawing at my insides. The world around me goes deathly still and I ignore the searing pain pulling at me as my joints pop and my bones slide into place.

Once my metamorphosis is complete I crouch low, putting my weight on my front paws in preparation as my nails rake the rich, pungent soil.

I take in all the eyes staring at me, one cruel set in particular. As coldness envelops me, fight or flight instincts kick in hard and my wolf lets loose a deep guttural howl, her control snapping like a frayed leash.

Targeting the master's challenging gleam in my crosshairs, my pewter eyes—eyes that have seen far too much for a girl my age—zero in on his pulsing jugular.

I draw the master's scent into my lungs, and when I move past the expensive cologne, I can smell the silver in his pocket, the gun powder residue on his hands from the last wolf he executed. Some small coherent part of my brain is telling me to salvage my plan, to show obedience in some last ditch effort to prove my loyalties, but I can't seem to leash my wolf.

She hungers to spill his blood and nothing or no one can stop her.

The rain falls harder, the torrential downpour coating my thick fur to my body and blurring my vision. Stone is yelling at me, his dark, hostile voice vibrating in my ears, cautioning me.

From my peripheral vision I can see him stripping his clothes from his body, desperate to shift back into his primal form. But I ignore his words of warning and bare my teeth in challenge. Despite the six guns pointed down at me, ready to shoot upon the master's signal, I call my wolf into action and my beefy paws sink into the mud. I take a threatening step forward.

My actions aren't rational, or smart, but when the strong, primal scent of wet earth reaches my nose and reminds my wolf of freedom, of running through the mountains unleashed, it prompts her to move faster.

Standing his ground, the master gives me a savage smirk, everything about his cool exterior exuding confidence. I realize it's his malicious way of letting me know he's not afraid of the runt he'd raised and controlled since birth.

As my enemy shows no fear in the face of an attack it occurs to me just how much danger I'm in. Just how much torture I'm going to have to endure before he kills me.

But I'm certainly not about to let that stop me.

4

As uncontrollable rage unfurls inside me, fury obscures my vision, causing me to miss the wolf closing in from behind. His heavy body lands on top of mine, and I crash to the ground with an agonizing thump. I thrash beneath him, my long talons digging into the wet, unforgiving ground as I struggle to gain purchase.

Sharp canines go to my throat and I howl, the sound carrying in the breeze and echoing off the distant mountains. Breathing hard, I twist and turn, wanting to see into the eyes of my killer before I draw my last breath. But when I manage to turn my neck, and find Stone restraining me from above, his teeth locked on my jugular with predatory precision, it has me questioning his loyalties.

But the ease at which he dominates me has my mind racing back to all the times the master pitted me against him during our agility training. I'm not sure why I'm suddenly thinking about such things. Perhaps it's because I'm dying and my very life is flashing before my eyes.

Regardless, as blood pours from my neck, one thing becomes glaringly apparent. Over the years Stone could have easily beaten me at the obstacle course, yet I always came out the victor. Everyone, the master included, thought it was because I was smarter, able to think with my head and not my heart. But I've only just come to learn that Stone has spent his life fighting with a combination of the two, and that has undeniably made him the better warrior. As I think more about that fact my heart crashes harder and suddenly everything becomes crystal clear.

Stone always let me win because winning meant I'd eat fresh food that day, even though he'd go on scraps. He let me win to save me, the same way he's saving me now.

"*Pride*," he warns and I don't miss the deep desperation in his voice as his warm breath washes over my face. When his familiar scent reaches my nostrils and weaves its way through my blood it does something to my wolf.

"*Stone...*" I cry out, wanting to tell him I'm okay, that I understand what he's doing, and that I'm grateful for everything he's done for me, but I can't quite find the right words.

He nudges me with his muzzle, and my spiked hackles settle when I meet his dark, pewter eyes—eyes that showcase so much emotion when they look at me.

He lets loose a relieved breath when my wolf finally simmers, relaxing beneath his careful hold. "*Easy, Pride*," he returns, the hostility gone from his tone as he shifts his body to ease the weight on top of me. "*Now follow my lead.*"

"Enough," the master demands and Stone instantly tenses. He obediently releases his grip on my neck, inches back and lowers his head in the company of the master.

"Well done, Stone." With that the master snaps his fingers and Mario appears with three collars.

I flip over and land on all fours, and when my attention flicks to Gem, my heart squeezes and the full impact of what I've done hits me. My rebellious wolf has put us all in great danger and I know in an instant I must fix it, must make it right. Otherwise all could be lost.

I'm not sure what finally made me snap, perhaps it was seeing Gem damaged, or our failed plan, or maybe it was master's evil smirk. But I do know that I'm angry, angry for losing control, for losing focus of my mission. But more importantly I'm disappointed.

How could I have lost sight of my goal?

I want to howl at my mutinous actions, for not keeping it together in the face of a crisis. Instead I give a savage shake of my head and berate myself for my behavior. I take a moment to remember my vow, remember that the elders died for me and I will not let their deaths go unavenged, which means that no matter how much the master taunts me, no matter how much I hate him, I can never, ever let my rage get the better of me again.

Panting hard, heavy rain drops drench my tongue and I widen my muzzle to drink them in. Hydrating myself in the downpour, I watch Stone shift back to human, and try not to cringe when my glance traces his deep purple scars. As he pulls on his jeans, I go on my haunches, taking that time to heal my battered body and settle my rattled mind.

Mario fits the powerful alpha with a collar, then comes to stand over me. I see trepidation in his eyes, and his hands shake slightly as they grip the circular metal band used to restrain me. That's when I realize the handler's not afraid of me, he's afraid for me.

He knows my fate.

"Shift," the master says, his voice so hard it hits me like a slap to the face. When I growl, he signals the other wolves in the courtyard to back away and resume their business. For them, the show has ended. Although everything in my gut warns that for me, it's just the beginning.

I watch them go, then my head jerks back to the master

and I slowly rise to my feet. As I think about the damage I've done, equal measures of guilt and worry come together in a heavy lump in the pit of my stomach. I have no idea if there is a way to repair the dent in our plan, or even if our army on the outside is still with us, but I do know that I'm the one who got us all into this mess, and I'll do whatever it takes to get us out. As I think about what it will take to tear down these walls and escape, I shake off my wolf and call on my human side.

A moment later I find myself standing in the courtyard stark naked, cold rain dripping down my body, and I become acutely aware at how vulnerable I feel. When I begin to shake, Stone moves closer, his large body protecting mine from those studying me with too much curiosity. As wolves move about and their soft, hungry growls echo in my ears, I keep my hands at my sides, refusing to show any sign of discomfort in front of the master.

A moment later Mario fits me with a collar, and it surprises me when he drapes my torn nightgown over my scarred body. I'm grateful for the small act of kindness, but know better than to comment on it.

With a snap of his fingers, the master gestures for Mario to leash Gem. Once he has the collar around her neck, the master says, "Take her to the east wing."

The east wing? Why would he have Mario deliver her to that remote part of the mansion? To where the master's private sleeping quarters are located? Why isn't he tossing her into the cellar with the rest of the wolves?

As I watch Mario lead her away my stomach knots. This can't be good. On no, this can't be good at all.

A shiver moves through me, tilting me off balance. I search the master's dark, weathered face for answers, and my blood drains to my feet when he offers me a knowing smirk. I continue to hold his gaze until his eyes narrows in displeasure.

With a crook of his finger he waves Lawrence over then steps closer to me, his face is drawn tight, the lines deeper then I remember. I can sense his impatience, the edginess brimming beneath the surface and I know it's not going to bode well for me. Tension coils through me as I harden myself.

Prepare.

His brow lifts and I know he's about to make an example of his rebellious wolf. After all, disobedience comes with a price. My muscles tense in anticipation and when the blow comes, it knocks the wind out of me. The hard fist to my stomach has me faltering backwards, and while my wolf wants to emerge, to retaliate, the bone-deep need to kill tugging at her hard, I keep her leashed. If there is ever a time I needed to submit and show compliance, it's now. Especially if I want to accomplish my mission. Something I have every intention of doing, because no matter what this man thinks, no matter what rules he plays by, I plan to come out fighting.

When his fist comes back again, Stone speaks. "I told her you still want to mate us. That's why she reacted."

The master's hand stills mid-air and he angles his head to see the alpha beside me. His eyes are cold and shrewd as they fix on Stone, a reminder that he's not a man to be toyed with and never, ever to be underestimated. "Are you telling me this to protect her?"

Stone's grin is wolfish, menacing, a boy who knows how to play the game better than most, I realize. "No. Never," he answers as his gaze leisurely rakes over my half naked body.

Everything in the way he's looking at me fills me with unease, and if I didn't know better, I'd think Stone was simply another one of the master's puppets, a wolf to do his bidding. But I do know better. He is deeply intelligent and is doing exactly what he has to in order to survive in this cruel prison. Exactly what he has to do to protect me from a brutal beating that would undoubtedly leave me scarred, inside and out.

Although something tells me the master hasn't even begun to discipline his defiant puppy yet. And no one, not even the powerful alpha who pretends to be broken will be able to help me when he does.

With renewed purpose, I lower my head in submission, knowing if I want to stay alive long enough to come up with a new plan, then I need to show obedience. As I stare at my mud coated feet, my heart tightens in my chest and I wonder how many times this boy is going to come to my rescue. How much abuse he's going to take because of me?

"I take it she's still putting up a fight?" the master asks.

Stone's dark bark of laughter reverberates in my blood and I try not to react when he trails a finger over my bare arm and says, "Yeah, but that's what I like about her. It will make breaking her that much more fun."

"Yes," the master says slowly, his lecherous gaze moving over my body before he adds, "She is a spirited one. Almost makes me want to do it myself, but since I need a purebred..."

As his words fall off, lingering in the air like a deadly bullet, Stone doesn't physically react, but I can hear his blood rushing faster through his veins, smell the anger bubbling inside him as his wolf bristles at the threat.

I keep my composure and remind him, "I'm a runt, remember. I can't give you purebred pups."

His voice is intense, the coldness in his tone chilling when he announces, "Nothing has changed, Pride."

"I brought back the rogue," I say.

At the mention of Logan, the master angles his head toward the private entrance leading to his office and scrubs his hand over his chin as he studies me. I resist the urge to shift my attention, but do wonder if that's where the master is keeping my mate.

"And you somehow thought that would make me change my mind?"

When I don't answer, the master puts his thumb under my chin to lift it. My hackles spike and I try not to cringe at the unwanted contact.

"Enlighten me," he demands.

I draw a breath and let it out slowly before I explain, "I thought if I brought the rogue wolf back in a show of loyalty you might change your mind. You said you wanted me to mate with Stone because I was too wild, too unpredictable and a cub would calm me. Doesn't my compliance prove I've settled? That I know my place?" I pause. Then for good measure add, "You once told me that I should be grateful because you keep us wolves safe. Well, I am grateful." I stop and shiver. "I don't ever want to have to run and hide from task force officers again."

"You were gone an awfully long time, don't you think?" His eyes scan my neck and I know he's looking at the puncture wound near my jugular. The spot where he'd once inserted a tracking device that is no longer there. "I was beginning to believe you'd run away."

"We were under attack. We had to go our separate ways," Stone intervenes and I realize he's saying it more for my benefit than the master's. It's his very careful way of corroborating our stories. But the truth is, I know Stone well enough to know how he thinks, and I was counting on him using that exact excuse. My initial plan depended upon it.

There is skepticism in the master's eyes when he responds with, "So you said." Stone opens his mouth but before he can speak again, the master hold his hand up to cut him off and zeroes in on the fresh scars marring his body. "What's interesting is that not even a proper beating could get him to change his story."

"Maybe that's because he's telling the truth," I say in an effort to defend the alpha.

The master pauses, his attention shifting to my body. "I wonder what truths I could beat out of you, or better yet..." Once again he angles his head toward his office.

As his voice falls off a second time, hot, black fear races through me and I don't miss the hidden meaning of his words. I'm intelligent enough to know that he's threatening Logan's safety, that he believes there is something between us —that he can use my empathy for the rogue wolf against me. I wonder how he'll try to do it, exactly what kind of pressure he'll apply.

My heart squeezes painfully in my chest and when his gaze narrows in on me I know exactly what he sees when he looks at me.

A monster.

But I know who the monster really is. If given the chance wolf shifters can lead regular lives. This man will always be twisted and evil.

My mother, as well as many of the other elders in the compound used to live normal lives until they were captured. They all used to be productive members of society and take to the mountains during the full moon in order to avoid hurting any innocent bystanders.

If only the world knew the truth. But how can I change the minds of millions? I'm only one girl. I can only take on one mission at a time, and currently that mission could mean the difference between life and death for every wolf in this compound.

As the master looks me over again—not a trace of soft-ness to be found in his sinister eyes—the rain slows overhead, the dark clouds scuttle by in a brisk, noonday breeze. The afternoon sun struggles to make a presence and when a long warm ray finally manages to break through and streaks across the courtyard, the master lowers his umbrella and I blink against the sudden brightness.

Once again the master's tone takes on a hard edge and he says, "You will be bred." He pins me with a glare, gauging my reactions when he adds, "One week from tomorrow."

When the moon is at its fullest.

My heart thunders, but thoughts of the full moon have me thinking of Logan and how he saved me from myself three weeks ago. I try to reach out to him, to connect, but my efforts prove futile. As I look into the master's hard face I wonder why he hasn't tossed Logan into the courtyard with the rest of us.

What does he want from him?

What will he do to get it?

Despite the years of hardening myself, there is nothing I can do to keep that worry off my face. The master opens his mouth to speak, but then stops to study me carefully.

I swallow and needing to get him to focus on something else I say, "If you don't need to tame—"

"Maybe I need you to breed for other reasons, Pride."

Why would he *need* to breed me?

He takes a threatening step closer and once again the hot stench of his anxiety washes over me like a deadly wave and turns my stomach inside out.

"Be thankful for that." He grabs my cheeks, squeezing hard, and puts his face dangerously close to mine, so close in fact, I can smell the coffee and cinnamon danish he'd eaten for breakfast. His voice drops an octave, as if to emphasize his next point when he says, "Because if I didn't need you, you'd already be dead."

With that warning hovering in the air and zinging through my blood like a hot bolt of lightning, he lets me go and turns to Lawrence. With a dismissive wave, he says, "Get her cleaned up and bring her to me. You know where I'll be."

Lawrence hooks my collar with a chain and shoves me from behind to set me into motion. My feet move in front of me, but they feel numb and cold—much like the rest of my body. As my mind races I no longer register the mud or gnarled roots tangling in my toes, no longer feel the uncomfortable wetness of my drenched nightgown clinging to my body.

All I can think about is how terribly wrong things have gone, and what I must do to fix them. I'd made a vow long ago and will stop at nothing until I free these wolves and crush the master.

Stone is talking to me, reaching out to me, but I block him—my mind is too chaotic to understand what he's trying to tell me—and the worry I hear in his voice simply makes me realize how desperate the situation has become.

But it's that desperation that fuels me on and has my brain strategizing my next move. I consider the kitchen and all its contents as I'm led inside, looking for something, anything that can help me.

Water drips from my body and pools on the floor, and Mica hurries to mop it up. Her eyes meet mine as she moves past me and I can tell she wants to say something, but with Lawrence watching she pinches her lips together tightly and obediently returns to her duties.

The enticing smells coming from the bubbling pot on the stove causes my stomach to grumble, but I ignore the aching discomfort as Lawrence leads me to Miss Kara's suite on the second floor. We move down the long hallway and I notice the house seems to be exceptionally quiet, the drone of the overhead lights, and the hum of the air conditioner piercing against the deafening silence.

I inhale as he leads me down the hall, searching for

Logan's warm, familiar scent, but the faint, memorable fragrance I catch instead has my senses going on high alert and my feet slowing.

No. It can't be!

I glance at the ventilation system overhead and a hot fireball of terror blasts in my stomach as the scent hits me with the force of a hurricane gale wind. Unlike the faint aroma the master used to bait me in the forest, this smell is strong, fresh and instantly takes my mind on a journey back to when I was just a pup, to when my parents coddled me in the nursery.

What if I'm wrong? What if he's not dead?

Papa?

5

My thoughts whirl out of control and my questioning mind races a million miles an hour as I'm led toward Miss Kara's suite at the far end of the hall, which suddenly seems to be closing in around me, causing my lungs to seize in the most painful way.

Could my father really be alive? Could he really be here? In the mansion? Or is this simply another sick way for the master to bait me. To break me.

My heart crashes hard against my chest and my insides reel as Lawrence nudges me along, my shoulder bouncing off the wall.

"What's the matter with you?" he taunts tightening my chain in his hand as my rattled mind wanders back to the past, to the very bitter day the master removed my father from his cell.

It might have been a long time ago, and I might have been a mere pup, but I remember it like it was yesterday. Remember my mother's hot tears running down her face, remember her valiant effort to comfort me when she was in desperate need of comforting herself. What I don't remember, however, is being led to the courtyard to watch the slaughter, nor do I remember hearing the gunshots reverberate off the distant mountains.

The master forces us to watch when he makes a kill, to teach us puppies that disobedience comes with a price. But he didn't bring us into the courtyard that day, which suddenly has me questioning everything.

Is it possible that my father hadn't been killed that fateful day long ago, that the master had a bigger purpose for him? If he's been alive all these years, however, why is he only resurfacing now, when the master is building himself an army to fight a threat I've yet to discover?

With my legs trembling and my mind focusing on those I've loved and lost, I stumble forward and push down the pain I cannot afford to feel.

But how can I possibly stop thinking about my father's scent? How can I possibly stop wondering if he's really alive or if this is simply the master's way of confusing my thoughts and keeping me off balance?

Then again, after experiencing freedom for the last three weeks, maybe being held captive again suddenly has me imagining things, conjuring up scents that aren't here. Maybe I'm simply losing focus of what's real and what isn't.

Either way, as Lawrence shoves open the double doors leading to Miss Kara's suite, I know I must put all thoughts of my father out of my mind for the time being. And the only way I can get through the next few hours is by convincing myself that the master planted his scent on purpose.

Otherwise, I'd be asking questions I might not want the answers to. Like why would my father have stayed away so long? Why wouldn't he have tried to come for me?

Because there are things you don't know, some inner voice whispers. *Things you're better off not knowing*. I think of Stone, and remember his warning that I shouldn't have come back, because it's too dangerous for me now. Could he have been talking about my father?

Disliking the dark path my thoughts are taking, and knowing I need to keep my head in the game if I want to win the war, I gather myself and concentrate on my surroundings. I can't let the master mess with my thoughts or shatter my hard-fought focus when survival dictates I look for a new way out of this prison.

I work to clear my head and tuck away my lingering worries as I step inside Miss Kara's suite. Now that the storm has passed, warm afternoon sunshine spills in from the big bay window overlooking her majestic mahogany desk but does little to chase the chills from my half naked body.

I take a small step into the room and the wood floor feels hard beneath my bloodied feet as I'm assaulted with a medley of floral perfumes. My nose twitches as I examine the large suite, looking for any kind of change, anything that could have been altered since my last visit, when Miss Kara fitted me in a gorgeous, white mating dress.

Looking as elegant and slim as ever with her long dark hair pulled back into an artful ponytail, Miss Kara lowers the book she's been reading and jumps from her plush recliner. Her eyes are bright, her arms wide as she rushes over to me.

She gives me a quick squeeze, then her peach-painted lips, full and glossy from too much makeup, pucker slightly. As she scrutinizes me, she pulls a long, wet strand of my dirty hair between her fingers for a close examination. Lawrence removes the chain but keeps my collar in place as she inspects my split ends, then she makes a tsking sound and turns her focus to my current bedraggled state. But suddenly pleasure moves into her eyes replacing the stern consternation as she takes in my new curves.

"Pride, look at you," she begins, her white teeth flashing in a smile. "You're growing up on me." Keeping her voice light, even though I know it holds a great amount of concern she asks, "How did this happen?"

I want to tell her it's because I'm no longer haunted by hunger, that for the last three weeks I've eaten real food—fresh food—but instead I just stare up at her and wonder how much the handlers and staff know about my escape. About what's going on inside the compound?

With that, she claps her hands together in a familiar gesture, and points a strict finger at me. "You might be filling out, young lady, but you're currently a pitiful mess." She waves her finger to the colonial door on my left. "To the shower with you."

As I move across her warm wood floor, I think more about Miss Kara. Besides Clover, she is the closest thing I've had to a mother since losing my own. Not only does she shower and dress us wolves when the occasion calls for it, she's also the one who teaches us about manners. In my line of work, education and manners come in handy when I'm trying to lure my mark.

Once inside the bathroom, I push on the door, leaving it slightly ajar like rules dictate. I peel my cold, wet nightgown from my shoulders, and drop it into the laundry basket, knowing I'll be given a new one by nightfall. Catching a glimpse of my reflection as I move past the mirror, I can't help but notice the changes in my body. But thinking of my body has me thinking of Sandy, and all the changes that are taking place inside hers.

Naked, except for the heavy collar around my neck, I turn on the hot spray and step inside the stall. I take a second to enjoy the blissful heat against my cold skin, then grab the strawberry scented soap as I think more about Miss Kara. Will she take her freedom if I offer it, or would she be too afraid of the consequences should I fail?

But failure is not an option, I remind myself.

After I shower, I wrap a big fluffy towel around my clean body and step into the room to find Miss Kara and Lawrence in deep conversation. My ears perk when I take in the distressed look on Miss Kara's face, and I try to tune into what they're saying, but when they see me they instantly separate.

Miss Kara rushes to me and leads me to her grooming station. She sits me in front of her big shiny mirror and brushes out my long hair before she trims the split ends. Her tone is light and conversational, and we discuss things like we normally do, talking about everything and anything except for my time in the woods. I wonder if she'd open up to me if Lawrence wasn't standing guard at the door.

Once she has my hair dried, she stands me up and I see a hint of worry in her dark, chocolate eyes as she reaches for her most expensive perfume and holds it just above my head. As she gifts me with a generous squirt, I don't take pleasure in the floral bouquet as it rains down on me from above. Instead I wonder why she's being extra generous today. She usually only sprays me with perfume when I'm being sent out to capture or kill a dangerous drug lord, one who dared to cross the master.

Since I know the master doesn't plan on letting me out of the compound anytime soon, this show of generosity worries me. It also begs the question, is she being nice because she knows the cruelties that lie ahead of me? Is this her small way of trying to make things easier for the master's rebellious wolf?

Once she's pleased with the state of my hair and makeup, she hands me a pair of jeans and a t-shirt—the master likes for his wolves to look presentable when we're brought to him. I pull them on, noticing how snug they feel now that I have curves. I don't, however, get shoes. Shoes have laces and I can make all kinds of weapons with laces.

Miss Kara puts her hands on my shoulders and turns me toward the mirror. Her eyes narrow in thought, a careful scrutiny as her gaze moves over my body.

"Look at you," she says in a soft voice meant for my ears only.

I stare at my reflection, which is almost unrecognizable— even to myself. As I wonder who that young girl is looking back, I note that my dark eyes, now lacking the inky black smudges beneath, no longer look stark against my skin. My long blonde hair looks healthy as it falls in wild waves around my face and I can't help but think how much I look like an ordinary seventeen-year old girl. One who would easily fit into the crowd.

But when I look closer, I see something else in my eyes, something that separates me from the teens I'd encountered when I was running in the national park.

"You look different."

That statement catches me off guard and fills me with worry. The last thing I want is for anyone to notice a difference in me. In this prison survival means blending in.

"I fed on wild game when I was lost in the woods," I hurry out. "I've put on weight."

Miss Kara shakes her head, and her ponytail swishes from side to side, slashing against her coffee-colored cheeks. "No," she says under her breath. "It's more than that, Pride."

I don't say anything. I can't. Because I know she's right. I also know that if she's noticing the slight changes in me the master will, too. Which means I'll have to work extra hard to desensitize and show no emotions in the face of the man I loathe.

"Pride?" she asks with quiet concern.

For the first time in my life I'm happy to hear Lawrence's voice when he interjects. In a lighthearted tone he uses only in front of Miss Kara, he questions, "Is there a problem, Kara?"

Miss Kara drops her hands and when she turns to him I grab an elastic band from her grooming station and stuff it into my pocket. I'm not sure what compelled me to do it. Perhaps it's because of Sandy. Perhaps if I can fix her hair or show her some small gesture of kindness, she'll see I'm not a selfish wolf who cares only about herself. Or maybe it reminds me of the girls I met while I was running in Olympic park, and that reminds me of freedom. And my mission to kill the master.

"No problem, Lawrence," Kara returns easily, her eyes cautioning me when she turns back to face me and fluffs my hair with a little too much enthusiasm. "Just a few finishing touches and then we're done."

But when I meet her glance in the mirror, and catch a whiff of her apprehension, I know she knows. She knows I'm going to take out the master. I tear my eyes away from hers because I can't allow anyone's fears to stand in my way.

I step away from the grooming station, and without so much as a backward glimpse, I move toward Lawrence. Silence ensues as he hooks his chain to my collar, and after he pulls open the double doors we retrace our steps back down the hall.

When we reach the main foyer, he doesn't lead me to the master's office in the west wing. Instead, we round the corner near the kitchen and take a back corridor until we come face to face with a heavy metal barrier.

Lawrence punches a code and the door slides open, and despite the precarious situation, my ears perk, deciphering the distinct sounds associate with each button. I store that information in the back of my mind as I examine my surroundings. My stomach tightens as I take note of the long cold, cement tunnel ahead of me, one I've never entered before and didn't know existed until now. Lawrence closes the heavy door behind us and the sound of his boots echoing off the walls sends shivers skittering down my spine.

I have no idea where he's taking me, and can't help but wonder what cruelties await me when we get there.

We come to the end of the hall, and stop in front of an elevator. Lawrence punches the button and when it arrives he shoves me inside. He puts his back to me as he punches in a code. He's trying to hide his actions, but I listen intently and take note of the sounds. A moment later we're dropping quickly, and I wonder just how far below the ground this elevator is taking us.

When it finally stops and the doors ping open I feel almost breathless, but I think it has more to do with the scent of fresh blood in the air, then the sensation of falling.

We turn a corner and walk up to another door, but before Lawrence reaches for the handle, he tugs on the collar of his T-shirt, and I can see the slight vibration in his hands. Despite the coldness in this dingy dungeon, beads of perspiration dot his skin and his chest rises and falls a little quicker.

His odd behavior has my hackles spiking, and when I note the uneasy way he's shifting on the balls of his feet, the way his Adam's apple is bobbing crazily as if going down for the third count, I draw in the rancid scent of his fear, and prepare myself for the worst.

As I fight down the chaos fighting for control inside me and desperately call on calm, I watch the handler run his damp palms through his hair. I realize that if he's this afraid, then whatever lies beyond that door is not going to bode well for me. Lawrence pulls in air, and puts on an expressionless mask before he turns the knob and readies himself to face the demons that haunt him.

When he finally pushes it open, the gruesome sight before me brings blistering, angry tears to my eyes. Hot, searing pain stabs at my heart and my throat aches painfully as I take in the horrific display.

I dig deep and try not to show a reaction, try not to give away my emotions but there is nothing I can do to keep my wolf from howling, my mouth from gaping open. Wild black fury erupts inside me, and every instinct I have warns that my next move in this deadly game of control could mean the difference between life and death.

Intense silence fills the room as all eyes turn on me. I struggle to keep my wolf leashed, struggle to stay standing when all I want to do is drop to the floor and weep, or better yet, shift and kill.

Saliva pools beneath my tongue and my stomach clenches. As acrid vomit pushes into my throat I realize that for the first time in my life, I know what real fear is.

6

With my gaze locked on the man I intend to kill, I bite the inside of my cheek hard enough to draw blood and wait for him to make the next move. As my stomach churns I force myself to breathe naturally, but when I draw air into my lungs, the scent of Logan's warm blood fills my senses and floods me with a confusing mix of anger and dread.

As the air ripples with tension, the aroma ripe and heady as it swirls around me, I realize I never should have agreed to this risky plan, never should have allowed Logan to place his trust in me.

I suddenly feel so powerless in the face of such violence, so defenseless and vulnerable that I can feel the strength drain right out of me. As I weaken, I instantly hate Logan for believing in me, for putting his life in my hands.

When my mate's rich, familiar scent trickles through my bloodstream my wolf gives an animal cry and I know in a heartbeat that the master has found my breaking point.

I wonder if he knows it, too.

Some small part of me had to expect this to happen. Yet

there was that other part of me, the part that hoped Logan would never have to face the master's wrath. But I should have known better. After all, my orders were to bring the rogue back alive, and there was only one reason the master hadn't killed the rebellious wolf on sight.

Logan has information and the master had every intention of getting it from him, using any means possible. And while we knew that fact coming back into this dark place, knew things could go very well go down this way, it still doesn't make the horrifying vision before me any easier to stomach.

"Pride," the master says, his tension palpable as he waves a hand toward the plastic chair across from his utilitarian desk, much different from the plush furnishings in his upstairs work station.

I don't speak. I simply move across the floor and gingerly lower myself into the hard chair as I listen to my heart thump wildly. Needing my focus more than I ever needed it in my entire life, I give myself a hard mental shake then peruse my surrounding, committing the entire dungeon to memory.

Unlike the master's luxurious office in the west wing, this one is icy cold. With no windows, the only source of light is coming from the single bulb overhead, a beaded chain dangling from the base. The walls are bare, the furnishing minimal, and the floor is equipped with drains, which makes this ugly space feel more like a meat locker than anything else.

Determination etched on his face and his voice lacking any sort of tolerance for me today, he announces, "It seems I have a problem, Pride."

I don't answer. I'm not sure if I can. With only the narrow metal desk separating us, I neatly fold my hands in my lap and stare straight ahead.

His chair scrapes the cement floor as he stands and everything about him screams danger. He walks to a small bar behind his desk and pours amber alcohol into a glass. I swallow as I watch him drain the liquid, then I nearly leap out of my chair when he flings the tumbler across the room, the glass shattering into a million tiny pieces.

"No more games, Pride," he warns, and acting purely on animal instincts I jump to my feet when he steps in front of me. A gun presses against the back of my head, and I don't need to turn to know Lawrence's lips are curled into a sneer, just waiting for me to make a wrong move. My jaw flexes painfully as I clench down hard enough to break teeth.

"No more games," I manage to choke out, finding it most difficult to keep my voice from sounding strained, to keep my body from giving away my raw emotions when Logan is less than five feet away from me, his eyes swollen, his jaw shattered, his beaten and battered body hanging from iron manacles.

The master perches himself on the end of his desk and nods to my seat. His voice levels out considerably when he says, "Good girl, Pride. Now I need you to tell me everything you know."

"I will," I say and carefully drop down into my seat and push as far back in the chair as I can, but I still can't seem to put enough distance between us.

"Pride..." At the sound of Logan's labored voice my gut twists with equal measures of grief and fear. Feeling light-headed as my blood rushes to my feet, I listen to his breathing for a moment. It's heavy and fractured, like he's broken a rib or worse, punctured a lung. I blink back the tears I cannot afford to show as panic invades my heart. If he doesn't soon shift and heal himself, I could very well lose him.

Knowing I can't let that happen, that I'll use any means possible to save him, I steal a quick glance at the boy who brought so much into my life. I can feel him reaching out to me, warning me to stay strong, to give away nothing. But how can I stay strong in the face of such ruthless torture?

How can I not?

The master jerks his head toward Logan. "I want to know where his pack is."

I take a moment to think about what Logan would want me to do, what he'd want me to say. While I can't bear for anything to happen to him, I know I can't let him down either. We've been through too much together for that. I pause for a long moment and consider Logan's state of mind and the number of bruises coloring his body. I understand the words I deliver next can put an end to his pain and suffering. But they could also damage an entire community.

My hands tighten into fists and I exhale a long slow breath, knowing what I have to do—what Logan would want me to do—but not liking it just the same.

"I have no idea where his pack is, or even if he has one," I answer with quiet confidence even though everything inside me is screaming in agony, my wolf begging me to kill the master and free my mate, but with the gun pointed at my head I know I'll be dead before I ever reach his throat. And if Logan can stay strong in the face of the master, then no matter how much it rips me apart inside, I have to stay strong, too.

For all our sakes.

The master's steely voice cuts through me when he grips my chin and his gaze is cynical when he says, "I thought we agreed on no more games."

"We did," I say unflinchingly as his fingers bite into my chin. He turns my face from side to side, studying me darkly, looking for some telltale sign of my deceit.

When Logan takes a deep shuddering breath, I know he can taste my fear. I stiffen, and work to harden myself, to leash my wolf because I can't show worry. Can't let the master know the bond we share. But it does give my wolf a measure of comfort to know that someday I'll let her off her leash, and let her do exactly what the master taught her to do.

Kill.

"Do you take me for a fool?"

"That would make me a fool," I say.

He lets go of my face and crosses his arms over his chest, the lapels of his expensive suit bunching under his arms. "Are you telling me that for the last three weeks, he never once mentioned his pack to you?"

"That's exactly what I'm telling you. I was concentrating on my mission, doing whatever was necessary to stay alive so I could get us back here to you."

"And did that mission mean running for three weeks?"

"I ran to avoid the paranormal task force. If they caught me, you'd never get the rogue." I try to sound casual and give an easy wave of my hand when I add, "So you can let him down. He's a lone wolf who doesn't know anything."

"He knew enough to get that tracker out of your neck, didn't he?" he challenges.

"That wasn't knowledge. That was luck." I roll one shoulder. "We were being hunted and I figured if he screwed up, I was dead either way."

"But you didn't die, did you."

It's a statement not a question, but I answer anyway. "That's because you taught me well. I knew it was a way for me to gain his trust and let him think I was on his side so he wouldn't run away from me."

The master glares at me, his eyes are dark, full of suspicion. "Maybe I taught you too well."

"Did you think he'd just follow me back here? I had no choice but to let him cut the tracking device out of my throat. I couldn't let him think I was leading him, or allowing hunters to follow us. He would have bolted for sure."

"Where did you get the gun, Pride?"

I lift my head like he should be proud of me. "I took down an officer and stole his gun, then I turned it on your rogue," I say, easily pushing the fabrication past my lips.

As he stares at me long and hard, I realize my scripted lies must be packing a punch, because even Logan looks worried. Like he might actually believe I'd led him back here on propose. But after everything we've shared, intimacies included, he knows me well enough to know that I'll do anything, *anything,* to ensure his safety.

Whether he likes it or not.

Just then I hear a noise outside the office. When the master looks past my shoulder, I wonder what all the commotion is about. The master makes eye contact with Lawrence. He gives a curt nod, a signal for the handler to open the door. Lawrence turns and I can hear his baggy jeans rubbing and his boots scuffing when he steps out into the hallway.

I slowly angle my head and catch him speaking quietly to Mica, not quietly enough to prevent me from overhearing, however. But it isn't what they are saying that holds my attention and has my stomach fluttering. Oh no, it isn't the food they are discussing that excites me, at all. It's what I see to the right of the door that fills me with hope and has my heart racing.

As the overhead light glistens on the rectangular security box hanging on the wall behind the door—its cover slightly ajar—I spot rows and rows of keys all lined up like obedient soldiers. I look closer and when I see one key, all shiny and new, I remember my padlock.

Could that be the key to my escape?

My mind races quicker than my heart as I plot and strategize a way to get my hands on it. But sensing the master's deadly gaze drilling into my back, I feign disinterest, turn toward him and keep my face neutral as I study my nails, the same way I once saw Gem do.

But thinking of Gem has my stomach knotting. I need to find her and free her from the master's clutches before we can make an escape. I can only assume he's keeping her close because of me, a token to hold over my head until he determines whether I've been broken or not.

Lawrence comes back and my stomach clenches in distress as he places a tray of sandwiches on the master's desk. Under the circumstances I couldn't choke one down even if I tried.

The master moves back to his seat and reaches for one. As he takes a generous bite, I wonder what kind of cruel, sick man nearly beats another person to death then washes down the blood on his hands with a cucumber sandwich.

"Have one, Pride," he says, his eyes gauging me.

Even though I suspect I'll only throw it up later, I know better than to refuse. When I reach for one, the master asks, "Who is the girl?"

"Girl?" I question, stalling as I work to come up with a reasonable explanation, even though I know full well he's talking about Gem.

"The one I found wandering around the estate."

It takes effort to chew my sandwich as my stomach tries to push it back into my throat. "I have no idea who she is."

"Don't you think it's odd that she showed up the same time as you?"

I don't for one minute think the master believes in coincidences so I say, "I think she might have followed us from the mountain."

He watches me chew for a long moment, then says, "Either way, I think she'll make a nice addition to the pack. Good breeding material."

Emotions press against my heart and I try not to show a

reaction as I take another small bite of my sandwich, then, even though I know I'm pushing it, I boldly ask. "Why are you impregnating all the females?"

He gives me an odd look, like Sandy's pregnancy means so little to him that it's not worth remembering, then he responds with, "Ah, you mean Sandy."

"Yes," I say, working hard to keep my anger in check.

His head nods with satisfaction. "I expect good strong alphas from her."

I use that opportunity to turn the conversation back to Logan. "Speaking of alphas, you probably shouldn't kill him," I say, trying to keep the desperation from my face, but I need to do something, anything to put an end to his pain and suffering. "He can give you good strong pups."

"You think so?" he asks, the corner of his mouth turning up in a knowing smile.

"I ran with him." I swallow so hard the sound carries in the bare room. "I know how powerful he is."

The master taps his fingers on his desk and shivers skitter up my spine when he gives a humorless laugh, one that reverberates off the walls and echoes around us. His deadly gaze bores into me when he says, "Interesting."

I want to ask what he finds so interesting, but shut my mouth when he gestures for Lawrence to release Logan. I take a huge bite of the sandwich to keep myself from crying out in relief. A moment later Logan drops to the floor with a resounding thud. He grips his ribs and a loud groan sounds in his throat, but he's still unable to shift and heal himself with his collar on.

Another noise sounds at the door and the master's eyes harden when he looks up to see one of his bodyguards standing there, a stricken look on his face.

The guard's uneasy glance goes from Logan, to me, to the master. "The perimeter has been..." he pauses as though unsure of how much to say in mixed company, then he lowers his voice and murmurs, "breached."

My heart leaps, wondering if it's my small army invading and hoping it's not. Our plan has been crippled, and now any attempt to overthrow the master with a direct hit will only end in disaster. We're in no position to fight. Not yet.

But when the master's furious gaze jerks to the bodyguard and he asks in a hard voice, "In broad daylight?" before he jackknifes out of his chair, I get the sense that he knows who's out there, and that such an attack has happened before.

Curiosity overriding fear, I watch him carefully, taking in the troubled look in his eyes as well as the beads of moisture dotting his forehead. Tension hovers in the air and when his face tightens wearily, I realize he instantly looks older.

I also realize I'm not the only one he's at war with.

My stomach grumbles softly as I listen to Sandy sleep restlessly beside me, my thoughts completely preoccupied with Logan. I play with the elastic band around my wrist and my heart squeezes painfully as I twirl and snap it. I can only hope and pray he's been placed in a cage free of his collar and allowed to shift, otherwise his fate will be sealed and there isn't a thing I can do about it.

It never fails to amaze me how strong my new mate is, how sure he is of me. The special bond between us warms me, and I know him well enough to understand that deep inside he believes I'll always make the right decisions. And even though I don't want to disappoint him, sometimes I hate the faith he put in me, because sometimes I'm not so sure of myself.

What if I can't always do the right thing?

Watching him suffer while I spilled lies that kept him in manacles was one of the hardest things I've ever had to do. I hope I never have to go through that again, otherwise I fear it could very well break me.

I scan my cell and pace quietly as I open my mind and try to contact Stone. I need to know what he knows and figure out what we're all up against if I want to put a new plan together to get us out of here. I also desperately need to know what's going on in the mansion, who is friend, who is foe, and who is waging a war against the master.

I sink to the floor and run my finger through the dirt. As I create pictures in the dust, a habit from childhood, I think about Logan and his promise to one day take me to the ocean. Will he ever be able to keep that promise? Or will the master destroy us first?

As my thoughts turn to the master, it has me considering his enemies. I'm smart enough to realize that something or someone is out there, threatening him and perhaps his drug cartel. He's building himself an army for protection. I wonder if the phantom enemy that is closing in from the outside has chased away my small army, or worse, captured them.

I think of Logan's family, the ones who came with us and the ones who stayed behind, and know I can't let the master get his hands on them. As the pieces of the puzzle begin to fall into place, it instantly becomes clear to me why Logan is so important to the master, why he wanted the rogue wolf brought to him alive—so he can harness Logan's family and add force to his numbers. And I can't forget that he's impregnating the females for that same reason. Werewolf pups grow fast and it doesn't take them long to learn how to fight. As I mull that worry over, I stifle a yawn as exhaustion pulls at me.

After a sleepless night my body is beginning to break down and I know I should rest while I still can, because I know the next few days are going to be difficult for all of us.

I push to my feet, step away from the impenetrable metal bars and force myself to lie down on my cot. As I stare at the wooden boards and scan the ventilation system overhead, my eyes slip shut and I work to regulate my breathing, but there is nothing I can do to stop my mind from recalling the distinct scent my sensitive nose picked up on in those very vents earlier today.

I lay there for a long time, my mind finally settling, but what feels like hours later, a noise at the foot of the stairs pulls me from my slumber.

I roll onto my side, unease exploding inside me and raising the hairs on my nape as I peer into the dark. As a tall figure emerges from the shadows and his face comes into full view, my heart crashes against my chest and the room begins to spin before my very eyes.

"Pride," the man says after a long time, and the sound of his voice, warm and familiar takes me back to when I was just a pup.

No! It can't be.

As old memories flood me, I rub the sleep from my eyes and wonder if I'm dreaming. Except when I blink my lids back open, he's still standing there, staring at me from the other side of my cage.

"Pride," he says again and my wolf howls in response to the urgency and emotion in his voice.

Feeling unstable, I tentatively climb to my feet, wondering if this is some sort of trick, some cruel way to break me. I track slowly to the metal bars and grip them hard, but when a warm hand closes around mine, my insides begin to quiver and I sink to the cold floor, my new nightgown dusting the dirty ground and washing away my picture as tears prick my eyes.

"Father?" is all I can manage around the lump in my throat. "Is that really you?" I ask, completely overwhelmed by the emotions pressing on my heart.

He smiles at me. It's warm, but cautious, and helps push back the chill in my body. I look closer, and take in the square shape of his face, older now, weathered, and more severe, like he's witnessed a lifetime of suffering. But it's his eyes when they lock on mine that has my heart aching and my throat closing in pain.

The hurt I see in the depths of his brown eyes, the regret shaping the outer edges twists me up with sadness.

What happened to him?

He sinks to the floor beside me. "Pride," he says. "I've missed you."

"I've missed you, too," I whisper. Somehow I find the strength to choke out, "I thought he killed you."

Darkness moves over his face, but I'm too numb to react. If the master didn't kill him, where has he been all this time? But I don't ask because some small part of me warns me not to, warns that I might not want to hear his answer.

His hand touches my face. "You've grown into a beautiful young woman." A long pause and then, "I always knew you would."

Unable to deal with the emotions his gentle touch brings, I try to cut the tension and mask my feelings by asking, "Are you telling me I wasn't born with my looks?"

With that he laughs and while the sound should be warm and comforting, it feels more like a blow to the stomach than anything else and generates a deep sadness inside me.

I've missed him so much.

"You were beautiful from day one, sweetheart," he assures me.

"Now look who's trying to be funny," I say, working to keep my voice from shaking as badly as my hands. "I was a gangly runt and you know it."

Humor leaves his voice when he says, "What I know is that you're a survivor, Pride. You always have been and always will be." His eyes go dark, serious when he continues. "Don't ever let anyone take that from you."

"I won't," I say when I see how solemn he's become, and I

feel a strange sense of relief when those two simple words bring a small smile to his face.

He holds my hand a long time, then breaks the quiet by asking, "Do you remember when you were little and I used to sing to you?"

I nod.

"Do you remember the words?"

As my mind recalls his whispered lyrics about love, loss and forgiveness, I say, "Yes."

"Good," he says and pats my hands. "That's good, Pride." Then I hear something in his voice, something that sounds like regret when he asks, "Do you remember the last words I spoke to you?" His voice hitches when he adds, "Before I left here?"

I swallow, and wonder what he's getting at. What is he trying to tell me? As I struggle to understand, to puzzle things out, I say, "Yes. You told me that some things are worse than death."

"Do you know why I said that to you, Pride?" He shifts closer, and when his comforting scent curls around me my heart tightens with long ago memories.

"To help me stay strong?" I answer, my voice sounding strangled, even to myself.

Anxiety fills his features and my body stiffens, everything inside me telling me I might not be ready for what he's about to say next. "Partly," he says, his voice falling off as we exchange a long look. But as I sit in silence, waiting for him to explain, he closes his mouth. As his lips form a tight white line I can't help but wonder if he thinks I'm not ready to hear it yet either.

But before I can ask him what else it means a noise above us has him stiffening. He presses a finger to my lips to hush me and slowly climbs to his feet.

He begins to back away from me, and I reach for him. "No. Don't go."

"Forgive me, Pride," he says as he steps further away, until he disappears into the darkness. "Sometimes we have to do what we have to do."

Breathing hard I jump up from the cold floor, my hand still outstretched as I frantically scan the cellar, my father's voice still lingering in the night even though I can't catch any remaining scent of him. My gaze darts from left to right, but when I find myself alone inside my cell, the basement empty except for Sandy, who is just beginning to wake, I let loose a cry.

It was a nightmare!

As that reality slowly sinks in I throw myself onto my mattress. I work to regulate my erratic breathing as my battered mind rushes in all directions, and I note the small part of me warning that it wasn't a dream at all, that my father really was here.

But it had to be a nightmare, I tell myself. It had to be. A bad dream that was brought on by yesterday's trauma. Otherwise it means my father has done something.

Something he needs forgiveness for.

But as a confined wolf who's been taught to trick and lure, I know nothing about forgiveness.

Except he wasn't here, I remind myself. None of this is real. It can't be. Swallowing uneasily, my shaky gaze goes to the door at the top of the stairs and I find it tightly shut, no signs that anyone has been in or out.

But no matter how hard I try to convince myself that it was nothing but a night terror, my stomach clenches with worry, because everything inside me is telling me that while my father might not have been here physically, he was still communicating with me.

As I think more about our exchange, I wonder what he is

trying to tell me, what he is asking from me. Despite my worn out body needing sleep, I'm suddenly too afraid to close my eyes. Instead, I lay there for the rest of the night, and run our conversation over and over in my mind until I hear the upstairs pipes groan awake.

A sign that the household is rising.

I'm thankful when the handler finally comes, and don't even care that it's Lawrence. All I want is to get out of my cage and get outside, to let the warm sunshine melt the ice inside me. Less than ten minutes later I find myself in the courtyard, the air fresh and crisp, the sky clear of clouds after yesterday's heavy rain storm.

I remain quiet, non confrontational as Lawrence removes my collar and I can see the way he's looking at me, wondering what's wrong with me. I know I should probably be sparring with him like I normally do, but I simply don't have it in me today.

Stepping away from the others and hoping to lose myself in the crowd, I look for Logan, unease zinging through my blood. When I finally spot him, dressed in a pair of worn jeans that hang low on his waist, my heart goes into my throat and relief just about has me sobbing. Except for the recent scars on his body he looks good, strong. Healed.

I try not to stare. I don't want to draw any attention to my rattled state. But when his eyes lock on mine and I see real worry lingering in their stormy depths, my stomach tumbles.

Does he know what happened to his pack? That the master has Gem?

I need to shift, so I can speak with him privately and find out what he knows. My hand goes to my new nightgown, but with all these wolves watching, I find it difficult to strip. As I consider that a moment longer I berate myself for my foolish behavior. The lives of many are hanging in the balance and it shames me that I'm worried about such a little thing like nudity.

When Logan sees me removing my clothes, he quickly sheds his own, and once we're both in primal form I saunter closer, not wanting my thoughts to be overhead by the others.

But before I can speak to him, Mario comes for him. The handler averts my gaze like he can't bear to look at me as he leads Logan to the obstacle course. I swallow hard and browse the yard, wondering who they'll put up against him. If I know the master, he's testing the alpha, testing his strength and stamina to determine if he's good breeding stock, which means there is only one other alpha he's likely to pit him against.

That thought has my stomach roiling. I spin around in time to see the master saunter into the yard. He looks hard, dangerous, a man on a mission.

He moves through his throngs of pets, examining them carefully and when I see him stop to look over Sandy, the way she stares up at him with adoring eyes doesn't go unnoticed by me.

Sick to my stomach at how broken she is, how she sees the master for something he isn't, I turn away, but not before I catch the brutal smile he aims my way. One that tells me he's up to something and it I'm not going to like it.

With my back to him I can tell he's watching me, I can feel his eyes cutting into my back. Feigning disinterest, I go down on my haunches and begin to groom myself, all the while trying not to show any sign of emotion when Stone is led to the obstacle course to compete with Logan.

Alpha pitted against alpha, they stare at one another, two strong, powerful wolves, both with sleek, streamlined bodies, ready to fight to the death. And while I know Logan is a wolf who can survive in the wild, he's playing in Stone's territory now, and that can't be good for any of us.

I see the way Stone is staring at him and I can feel the rage emanating off his body, the conflict between them escalating in the close confines. His long talons dig into the soft earth and his growl rumbles like thunder and hovers over the courtyard like a dark cloud as he sizes up his enemy.

They're staring at one another, two blazing sets of pewter eyes ready to set the compound on fire, but there are too many wolves milling about, their collective voices interfering with my ability to hear what they are saying to each other. From the look in Stone's eyes, however, I can tell he's out for blood.

With the master watching I can't do anything. I can't canter over there and tell Stone to simmer, otherwise we might never get out of here. I need those two working with me, not against me if I want to get into the master's dungeon and get the key that could very well be the answer to our escape.

When the starter gun sounds, I hold my breath, half expecting Stone to go for Logan's throat instead of running the course. But alpha that he is, I realize this is his chance to show domination over my mate, and he's not about to miss that opportunity.

After all, there can only be one alpha in the pack.

Stone flashes white canines as his beefy paws dig into the dirt, bloodlust flashing in his pewter eyes. With power, agility, and practiced ease, he darts forward and jumps the first hurtle. He slowly climbs the ladder, Logan's powerful legs pushing hard as he keeps pace beside him. Using their sharp teeth, they both clamp down hard on their ropes, their jaws bearing the entire weight of their bodies as they swing across the mud pit in sync.

I glance ahead, my eyes scanning the equipment and looking for a flaw in the course, one Logan isn't bound to notice. How could he, really, especially when he's not privy to the cruel tricks the master likes to play on us? It doesn't take long for me to see the defect in the zig-zags.

When I notice the thin layer of green sod strategically placed over a newly bulldozed hole, I instantly know it's a trap. I also know if Logan lands in it he could very well break his neck. The master likes to point out that these manmade traps help keep us on our toes and keep us alive and that he's simply doing us a favor by sharpening our skills so we're always at the top of our game.

My heart pounds faster and I make my way closer, my small body weaving around the wolves pacing the compound, and I know the rapid fire rushing of my blood can be heard by all. As Logan approaches the trap, I can't help myself. I make a noise, a half cry, half howl.

That's when Stone turns his attention to me, my distress signal gaining his focus. With his gaze diverted, he missteps, his ankle catching the outer edge of the trap, and his hard body lands with a painful thump. I suck in a quick breath, and see how furious he is when Logan jumps over the trap and takes the lead.

A hush falls over the crowd as Stone's low growl rents the air. He pulls himself from the hollowed-out hole and he gives a savage shake of his head as his eyes zero in on Logan's position. A moment later he bolts forward and instead of running through the long tube ahead of him, he jumps on top of it, and pounces on Logan when he exits the tunnel.

My insides twist and a shiver skips down my spine as he goes for Logan's throat. Using swift, agile movements I try to get closer, to communicate with them, but the master is watching me, waiting for me to do something, anything.

I stand still, knowing any more action on my part will be a dead giveaway and the last thing I want is for the master to know how I feel about these two. As I maintain calm on the outside, fury erupts inside me and it's all I can do is swallow it down. Tormented by the sight of the two wolves in a bloody fight, my body tenses and I clench down hard on my jaw as I watch them rip into each other, and all the while I stand idly by unable to do anything about it.

Logan retaliates, his powerful muscles bunch as his nails slash at Stone's face, the fresh scent of blood causing a frenzy among the other wolves. I listen to the gruesome sound of claws tearing flesh and strong bones crunching like glass. A ball of dry dirt forms a dark cloud as the two tumble along the ground in a mass of black fur and fangs.

I steal a glance at the guards above, wondering how long they're going to let this battle go on. From their smirks, as well as they way they are exchanging knowing nods, I get the impression that not only did they expect this, they're betting on the outcome.

As panic invades my stomach, I pull in a quick, sharp breath and fight down a strangled cry. I know I need to put a stop to this chaos before they kill each other. But before I can do anything, Logan pins Stone beneath him, his big paws holding his shoulders down. Stone's dark, wild bark of fury echoes off the mountains and using his back legs he tries to kick the alpha off and gain purchase.

My skin prickles because I know Logan is in "kill or be killed" mode, and I fear he's about to puncture Stone's jugular and let the life bleed out of my childhood friend right before my eyes. A pained expression rips across Stone's muzzle and somewhere behind me I hear a soft, hungry growl as the cannon thunders on the mountain.

As I watch the violence, I can feel my own blood draining. With the situation becoming dire, completely out of control, I know I have to do something. I'm about to make a move, but the master steps up beside me, his large body casting shadows over my small animal frame. I'd been so caught up in the fight, so worried about the outcome that I hadn't even heard his approach.

Not smart for a wolf with a mission.

His hand rakes over my fur, smoothing down my hackles and since I can't stand his touch, I shift back to human, hurry to my nightgown and pull it back on. Once I'm dressed the master moves close.

"It seems our rogue is a powerful one, after all," he says as he comes to a stop beside me.

I don't look at him. I can't. Party because I can't stand the sight of his face, and partly because I'm so focused on the fight—on the amount of blood being spilled—that I'm unable to peel my eyes away.

"I told you he was," I say between grit teeth.

From my peripheral vision I watch the way the master folds his arms across his chest and rocks back on his heels, an irritating habit he has. "Now why do you suspect they're fighting, Pride?" he asks, and I know he's baiting me.

I angle my head and give him a defiant look, one that suggests he's dense, and when I meet his evil eyes, a black wave of darkness churns inside me, pulsing, rising to dangerous proportions until my wolf is clawing at my insides.

My wolf howls and she doesn't care about the punishment that will come with my next words when I deliver them. "That's what happens when you put two alphas in the same yard. Surely you expected this," I challenge.

He glares at me, his annoyance palatable. The taste of his anger settles on my tongue as I wait for the hard slap to the face, but it doesn't come. Instead he looks past my shoulder and gives a nod to the guards. I resist the urge to exhale a relieved breath and instead roll my tongue around my dry mouth when I hear gunshots crack the air.

A moment later the two wolves separate, both breathing hard as they continue to circle one another, baring their sharp fangs. Saliva drips from their muzzles, and their fur is a tangled mess of dirt and fresh blood, but neither one is quite ready to back down.

Gun in his hand Mario steps up to them, his footsteps are slow and cautious as the wolves watch each other, both panting heavily. Clearly Mario is smart enough to know better than to place himself between two feuding alphas. He's speaking to them, using words meant to calm. Logan is the first to shift back, and I'm proud of him for it.

Once they've both returned to their human form, they stand at their full height, and Mario fits Stone with a collar. He gives the alpha a hard warning glare before he tosses him a pair of jeans and shirt. For a minute I wonder if Mario is trying to tell him something. For a minute I wonder if they're on the same team.

The master slants his head and a dark, warning shiver pulses heavy in my blood as he slides me a dangerous look. He has a strange calmness about him but underneath it I can smell his excitement. It's a scent that always worries me.

He gives a slow, easy nod of his head and his voice is deceivingly mild when he announces in a tight tone, "You're right, Pride."

Not liking the sound of that at all, I wait for him to continue but when the words don't come I narrow my eyes and meet his challenging gaze with one of my own before I come right out and ask, "I'm right about what?"

His eyes fasten on me, dark, dangerous and deceptive—a gleam shining in their evil depths.

"There can only be one alpha in the courtyard."

8

"*There can only be one alpha in the courtyard.*"

As the master's words bounce around inside my head like a pinball, my brain takes a moment to decipher the meaning. I feel myself go pale and briefly close my eyes in distress as a violent wave of anger cruises through my bloodstream at breakneck speed until hot steam is all but rising off my body.

With my pulse jack hammering, my queasy stomach rebels in protest and I'm certain I'm going to vomit. Because I know at once he's going test me again.

Before I can ask what he plans on doing, he twists on his the balls of his shoes and makes his way toward the private entrance leading to his main level office.

I stare at his retreating back, studying the casual way he moves. Without conscious thought, my eyes go to the six guards overhead. With their attention diverted, occupied by the fight between Logan and Stone, I take a moment to calculate how long it would take me to reach the master. Could I rip his black heart clear from his body before the guards turned their deadly guns on me?

Even though I know it wouldn't be a wise move on my part, it still doesn't stop me from considering it, or from playing the scene out in my mind's eye. But as I run the scenario through my thoughts, I hear Stone inside my head, calling out to me.

I turn in time to see him approach, and catch the careful way he's looking past my shoulder to ensure the master is out of the courtyard, unable to watch or hear our exchange.

My focus goes to Logan, who suddenly seems to be lacking his calm steadiness as Stone approaches me first. My ears twitch as Mario fits my mate with a collar. Once Logan is leashed, he climbs into his jeans, pulls on a t-shirt and makes his way toward me, each step determined, purposeful.

"*Pride*," Stone says in an attempt to pull my attention back to him.

I tilt my chin and blink against the glare of the sun as I stare up at him. "*What was that all about?*" I demand.

His eyes darken. "*You know what it's about.*"

"*It wasn't Logan's idea to come back here. It was mine*," I remind him.

Logan steps up to me, and in a possessive move, he nudges up against me as if to lay claim to his mate, and when Stone's nostrils flare I know I have to take charge of the situation before it gets out of control again.

I inch away from the crowd until the brick wall is at my back. The two alphas follow close behind.

As they flank me, I turn to Logan first and speak in whispered words. "If we're going to get out of here all three of us have to work together."

He gestures with his chin. "Tell that to him. He's the one who attacked."

I know he's right and I also know I'm not about to lay blame or begin a debate on who started the fight. We have more pressing matters. Instead, I lower my voice even more and ask, "Do you have any idea what happened to your pack?"

His mouth turns down in a frown and he drives his hands into his pockets as he gives a slow shake of his head. The concern on his face makes what I have to say next so much harder. With no easy way to tell him, I try to soften my words as much as possible before I announce, "He has Gem."

Darkness mingles with worry and I can see a storm brewing in the depths of his ocean blue eyes. "Something must have gone seriously wrong."

"There's something out there," I rush out. "I saw someone or something on the monitors."

Logan's frown deepens and he angles his head as if listening to a distant sound. "What do you mean some*thing*?"

I think about the large black, cat-like animals I spotted prowling around the mansion and turn to Stone. "Do you have any idea what's going on?"

He rolls one shoulder. "We're kept in the dark, but I do know the master is creating an army."

"Who is he at war with?"

"Just stop for a minute, Pride."

I stare at him and wonder what he's getting at.

"Just breathe," he says as his nostrils widen to draw in air.

I'm not sure if he's trying to calm me, or if he's trying to show me something. I'm about to ask, but when he says, "Just do it," I take a moment to pull the surrounding scents into my lungs. I move past the rich moist earth, the sweet aroma of grape juice, as well as the pungent smell of gun powder still lingering in the air.

I go deeper and that's when I smell it. Musky. Skunky. Foul. My eyes widen because I know there is only one animal with such a stench, one animal that can rouse the wolf inside of me.

Cat.

My wolf howls and claws at me, eager to take chase.

With my mind racing, trying to get a grip on things, I look at Stone. I remember what I saw on the monitor, and those were no ordinary house cats. Could there really be...

"What are they?"

"*Panthers*," Stone says, his answer for my ears only.

I gave a perplexed shake of my head. I know I've been compounded all my life but I'm not naïve to think werewolves are the only supernatural beings on earth. But panthers?

"How? Where?" I ask, not wanting to exclude Logan from the conversation.

"*I don't know.*"

"What?" Logan asks cautiously, his uneasy gaze darting between the two of us.

My voice is unsure, hesitant. "Those things out there. I think they might be panthers," I say, dumbfounded. "How can that be? I've never heard..."

Logan's brows furrows and my words fall off because I can tell he knows something I don't. "We need to find Gem and get out of here."

The urgency in his voice has my stomach cramping. "What is it?" I ask.

He goes quiet for a moment, and then says. "There are rumors about other animals being able to shift to human, like us."

"Panthers?"

"Yeah, panthers," he says. "Among other species." Then he softens his voice when he sees my astonishment. I can tell he wants to come closer, to wrap his arms around me, so I turn my head away to stop him. "You've been sheltered, Pride. Having been in this compound your whole life, you have no idea what really goes on in the world."

I look back at him. "Miss Kara—"

"She doesn't teach you everything. Only what your master wants her to and besides there are things you won't read about in any textbook." He nods toward the brick wall at my back. "Things the PTF don't want to get out."

"Such as?"

"For one, there are many paranormal beings out there and two, the officers don't hunt just wolves."

"Tell me more," I say as I imagine what other kinds of shifters exist. Where do they live? How do they survive? Are they friend? Or foe?

"What I understand is this: these shape-shifting panthers aren't from around here and they run purely on instinct. To make matters worse, the human part of them lacks our sense of right and wrong. This makes for a very dangerous enemy."

Shivers skid down my spine and I lean forward to brace my hands on my knees. I slowly exhale. "Meaning, they're deadly."

"I remember overhearing Malcolm talking about them when I was younger," he continues to explain. "While these cats are deadly, he did point out they lived alone in the African jungle and bothered with no one but themselves, but he also said if they were ever captured and harnessed, the world would be in a load of trouble."

I stand back up, understanding that this presents a whole new set of problems for us. "If we figure out their weaknesses we can figure out how to defeat them. Clearly someone has found a way to gain control over them."

"It's dog against cat," Stone says. "How bad can that be for us?"

Logan's brow rises. "Lethal, considering cats have nine lives." He looks at me and I take that time to wonder who is controlling them and what they might want with the master. Had these panthers chased away our small army, or had they

—? I shut my mind down, refusing to go there, refusing to believe it could be true.

"Do you have any idea where Gem is?" Logan asks.

"The master put her near his quarters and is keeping her close. I can only assume he's distancing her because he suspects she's with us."

"We can't break out of here with her still trapped," Logan says.

"And exactly how do you plan on breaking out of here? Do you have a new plan?" Stone asks, his voice challenging, skeptical.

"I do," I announce and they both turn to stare at me. "Well not a plan exactly, but a crucial first step in figuring one out." At least I hope it is. Equal amounts of confusion and shock spread across their faces when I add, "It requires me getting back into the dungeon."

Logan's body stiffens as he stares at me long and hard, and I know he's thinking about his own horrific experience in the dungeon. "Why?"

"What do you mean *why?*" Stone barks out and once again I feel his mounting rage. "She's not going anywhere near that room, for any reason."

"Stone—" I begin, frustration mushrooming inside of me as I cut him off with a glare.

Logan steps closer to me in a show of protection and his voice is low, concerned, when he says, "Tell me why, Pride. What's in that room?"

With tension visible in his posture, Stone cuts us both off and stares at Logan's fresh scars. "Are you kidding me?" he barks out.

Logan bares his sharp white teeth, a warning for the other alpha to back down. "We need to listen to her."

Stone gives a hard shake of his head and adds, "For a guy who's just been subjected to a round of torture, I can't believe you're actually entertaining the idea of letting her walk into that hellhole." Stone runs unstable hands through his dark hair, mussing the ends before continuing, "Do you have any idea what will happen to her if she gets caught."

"Pride," Logan says, uncertainty flickering in his eyes as they focus on me. His worried gaze moves over my face. "Talk to me. Tell me what's in that room?"

My heart quivers, because after everything Logan has been through because of me, he's still willing to believe in me, to put his future, his very life, in my hands.

I'm not sure I deserve such faith because I'm not sure I can live up to it. I keep the emotion from my voice when I answer. "It's where he stores the keys to the compound. I think I spotted the key to my cell."

His blue eyes narrow carefully. "You can't think, Pride. You have to be sure."

I steady myself. "I am sure and I have to get in there."

"And once you free yourself, where are you going to go? What will you do? We'll all still be caged."

"I want to get to Gem. To find out what she knows and figure out a way to free her before we come up with a new plan and try to break out of here."

"How can you get to her? The house has motion sensors."

"Through the vents," I say.

Logan smiles at me. It's warm and soft and so full of unfettered pride that my heart tightens with emotions. "See, sometimes it really does pay to be small," he responds.

For a moment I think about how much Logan taught me —about myself and about the world—while we were running in the park. If it wasn't for him, I never would have thought of my size as a strength instead of a weakness.

"Maybe she can tell us what happened to your pack." I take in the wall surrounding us. "With any luck they're still out there waiting for some sort of signal from us."

Logan frowns. "I don't think so, Pride. I've been trying to communicate but can't reach any of them."

We both go quiet for a moment, thinking things over and I can't help but feel both sad and guilty. How will I ever live with myself if something happened to them because they were trying to help me?

"I can't believe I'm hearing this." Stone turns on Logan again. "And I can't believe you actually let Pride return here. She had her freedom." He drives his finger into Logan's chest, provoking him. "You should have ensured she kept it. You're a sorry excuse for an alpha."

Logan's nostrils flare, and I can feel his wolf pacing, his every movement threatening. "Don't push me, Stone," he warns, keeping a level head as Stone taunts him. "It's not the time or place for this. And Pride is stronger and smarter than you'll ever know. She can make her own decisions, and as her mate, I'll support her in whatever she decides."

"How can you possibly call yourself her mate?" Stone scoffs. "A *real* mate is supposed to protect, not let her walk straight back into danger."

Something in the way Stone says *real* catches my attention, and takes me back to my time in the woods with Logan. I think about the way Logan reacted when he first learned that I could speak telepathically to Stone in human form. As my hackles rise I wonder exactly what's going on here. What do they know that I don't?"

"Stone," Logan warns, his teeth gritting in anger, challenging the alpha with an unwavering stare. "I *am* her mate."

Stone's eyes go suddenly black and the sound coming from the depths of his throat is low and menacing, portraying his every dark emotion. His lips twist and the two share a knowing look, one that disturbs me and has me questioning everything.

"Right," Stone responds and then my heart punches into my throat when he adds, "Except we both know otherwise."

With that Logan's control snaps and he hurls himself at Stone, delivering a hard punch to the alpha's jaw. Stone flies backward, and hits the ground hard, the sound thunders in the air and prompts me into action.

Like Mario, I'm smart enough to know that getting between two alphas in the middle of a dog fight isn't an intelligent move, but I need to neutralize this situation, partly because they're drawing unwanted attention and partly because I want answers and I want them now.

"Stop," I say to Logan, holding my hand against his chest before he pounces again, then I turn on Stone as he climbs to his feet. The look on his face is so intense, so dangerous I almost forget how to breathe. But the anger still can't mask the hurt I see beneath that outer shell, a deep sadness that has my heart squeezing.

"What are you talking about? What do you both know?" I demand.

My nerve endings tingle as Stone rubs his jaw, his black eyes locking on Logan's. I try to tap into his thoughts but he's blocked me and for a minute I'm not sure he's going to tell me what they know and I don't. Then as if to taunt my mate and provoke him even more than he already has he opens up his thoughts and speaks to me telepathically.

"Why do you think we can communicate like this, Pride?"

My heart starts beating faster and as the truth begins to unravel inside my brain I can't believe I hadn't figured it out before now. The courtyard sways in front of me, my vision going a little fuzzy around the edges, and it forces me to lock my knees to keep myself upright.

No. It can't be...

"Yes it can be and it is," he responds, still tapping into my thoughts.

I push him out of my head and build a defensive wall around my thoughts before my gaze flies from his face to Logan's. Logan's back goes straight and there is a weariness about him as I glare at him in challenge.

"Did you know this?" I ask, my voice trembling, my throat tight with emotion.

"Pride," he reaches for me, his eyes filled with tender concern as the hard angles of his face soften. But it's that sorrowful expression in his eyes that makes him so transparent and tells me everything I need to know.

Confusion and anger come at the same time and I step back, needing to distance myself as my mind races, trying to wrap my brain around this new information and what it might really mean for all of us.

"Logan," I choke out, my heart picking up tempo as I give a perplexed shake of my head. By small degrees his body tightens and his hands fists at his sides. I see concern reflecting in his eyes when they meet mine. It shocks me that Logan knew all along that only *true* mates can speak telepathically when in human form and he purposely kept that information from me.

I realize that while I'm just learning about love and trust, I thought mates, *true* or not, were supposed to be open and honest with each other.

"Why didn't you tell me?" I question, trying to keep the hysteria from my voice as I watch a deep sadness invade his blue eyes. As I study him, I realize that for the first time I see something in Logan I've never seen before. Real fear.

But I'm not sure how I feel about all these secrets and I know I'm not prepared for the mix of emotions they bring. All I know is that my stomach is sick, my head is spinning and well...okay, maybe I do know how I feel. Foolish. I should have known better. I should have figured it out.

"*Don't beat yourself up. I kept you in the dark about a lot of things. In this place it was for your own good.*"

"Don't," I say to him out loud, wanting to sever the intimate connection, and hating that he kept things from me. Important things. Things that might have made a difference.

Or might not have.

But those decisions were mine to make, not anyone else's.

As conflicting emotions rush through me, the starting gun sounds again and pulls my attention. It's a reminder that I have more important matters to worry about right now. I shake my head to clear it. I can't be worrying about who my mate is and who he isn't when I have more pressing concerns like how I'm going to sneak into the master's dungeon and get my hands on those keys.

And I need these two backing me if I want to pull it off without getting caught.

"*I'll go*," Stone says, and I realize he's reading my thoughts.

I turn on him, and say, "You know as well as I do that I can get in and get out quicker than you. Besides I need you both to cause a distraction to keep the handlers and guards busy."

"How do you know which key you'll need?" Logan asks as he peruses the courtyard, everything in his expression letting me know he's looking for potential danger.

"I have a new lock."

"Right," Stone says, his voice tight as he kicks at a rock.

My head jerks to him. "What do you mean *right*?"

With his back to the wall, he bends one knee and presses the pad of his foot to the stone barrier. He looks away from me for a moment, breaking eye contact, and I get the sense the next words are too painful for him to deliver. He draws in air, slowly turns back to me, and says, "Jace broke it. When they were taking him..." he swallows before he says, "away."

I shudder involuntarily and blow out a shaky breath.

Stone doesn't have to say what 'away' really means for me to understand, and I'm glad he doesn't voice that awful truth because I'm not sure I can bear to hear it. I choke down the emotions clogging my throat and think more about Jace and Clover, the elders who died to give me freedom. Both warmth and sadness touch me, because I know any sort of disobedience on Jace's part is out of character. No, he broke that lock for one reason and one reason only.

Me.

Everything inside my gut tells me so.

I look at Stone, and while he might think the elder wolf snapped the lock in a fit of rage, I know he didn't. Somewhere deep inside, Jace knew I'd be back and this was his way of giving me an advantage, something that could hopefully help aid in my escape.

And I'm not about to let him down.

Clearing my mind to focus only on the task at hand, I turn my back on the two alphas. "I need to go," I say, and casually walk away before either can put up a fight. "You two do what you need to do."

I inch my way along the perimeter and make my way toward the mansion. A moment later, I hear a shout and the ground practically shakes beneath me as I slip inside the kitchen door. I feel a slight sense of relief to know the two boys are causing the distraction I need, instead of trying to stop me.

Mica turns to me, and for a moment my heart stops. She's always been kind to me, but she's also under the master's control. I hold my breath and wait. Will she scream? Will she call for a handler? Will this be the end for me?

With no time to waste, I keep my eyes on her and begin to pad softly along the cool tile floor. As she watches me, dark lashes blinking over cloudy eyes, our gazes lock in a silent battle. The last thing I want to do is to get her into trouble for my disobedience, but the only route I know to the dungeon is through her kitchen.

My hands brush along the wall as I feel my way along, and when I see some small part of her give, relief rushes through me. Her head inclines slightly, and she gives me a gentle nod of understanding before she turns back to her baking. With her back to me, I take the corner quickly and move toward the heavy door leading to the elevator.

Remembering the distinct sounds associated with each number, I punch in the code and my heart practically breaks through my chest as the door slides open. With desperation outweighing fear of getting caught, I peruse the long hallway, looking for threats before I dive in.

After determining all is clear, I move with speed, my steps quick as I slip into the corridor and retrace my earlier path back to the elevator.

I press the button and crouch low as I wait for it to reach me. When it finally comes I slip inside and as I punch the key to the bottom floor, I try to not to notice the quickening of my pulse, the sweat on my hands, the fear inside me. Needing a distraction, I pull the elastic off my wrist, quickly braid my hair to get it off my face and secure it with the rubber band.

My head spins as I descend, and when the elevator comes to an abrupt halt, I can feel the air seize in my lungs. The door isn't opening. Why isn't the door opening? I examine the tight space, and keep the panic at bay as I work to figure out my next move, but when the doors finally spread to reveal the master's underground chamber, I draw in a sharp breath.

I climb out, and move urgently down the hallway until I'm standing outside the master's dungeon. I search the walls for monitors and try to keep one step ahead of them. I carefully inch open the door and the hot familiar scent of blood curls around me.

Logan's blood.

As it stings my eyes I choke on it, and press my nose into the crook of my elbow until I can get my revolting stomach under control. I don't bother to turn on the light. I don't need to. Working quickly before I get caught, I inch the door closed behind me but when I find the lid on the metal security box closed and locked, my heart goes into my throat.

No!

Thinking quickly, I shift my focus, looking for a key, or any sort of object that I can use to jimmy it open. With an uneasy feeling curling around me, I hurry to the master's desk and pull the drawers open, cringing as the metal groans in protest.

I search through the contents, pushing papers aside, but my hands slow when I see a familiar piece of fabric, the same fabric the master used to bait me in the woods. I pull it from the drawer and press it to my nose. As my father's fresh scent fills my senses, my wolf howls.

Why? How?

But with the very threat of getting caught hovering over me, I have no time to consider it longer. That's when my hand connects with something cold. I grip the key in my palm and rush to the box, hoping and praying it fits the lock.

When it slides in I give a silent prayer of thanks. I work quickly, my eyes scanning the rows of keys until I come to the brightest and shiniest. I slip it from the hook, curl my palm around it, and relock the box. Then I rush back to the master's desk to ensure everything is back in place.

Once I have everything in order I take a quick look around. With no windows in the dark dungeon I'm unable to tell what's going on in the courtyard. Are the two alphas still causing a commotion or have things settled? If they've settled will the handlers notice my absence and come looking for me?

With that thought urging me on, I close the master's

door, and bolt to the elevator. I stab the button and don't stop to consider why it's not already there waiting for me.

I press my palm into my stomach and take deep, slow breaths to calm myself, my hand holding the key close as I await the elevator's return. I almost breathe a sigh of relief when I hear it come to a grinding halt.

But when the doors ping open to reveal a set of eyes full of anger I stop breathing. And when those dark eyes fix on me, my stomach lurches with panic, because the look in those dark, intense eyes is beyond frightening and I know in an instant, I'm in serious trouble.

9

"What do you think you're doing?" Mario asks. But before I can answer he looks past my shoulders to take in the narrow hallway and I know he's trying to determine what he's up against. When he realizes I'm alone he zeroes back in on me.

I take a small distancing step back and balance on the balls of my toes as my survival instincts kick into full force, screaming at me to make a clean kill and save myself. But Mario is only doing his job, I quickly remind myself, and he's trapped inside this prison every bit as much as I am. Killing him would make me no better than the master or any other drug lord who harbors wolves to do their dirty work. Those are the ones that need to be stopped and killed—every last one of them—not the handlers who are simply marionettes under their control.

"I got lost," I say for lack of anything else and note how breathless I sound, the threat before me rousing my wolf. I realize it's a poor excuse but my brain is currently on hyper drive and under the circumstance I'm unable to come up with anything else that might sound credible. Not that I think my sad excuse is in anyway believable, however.

Mario braces one hand on the rubber track running the length of the elevator door to hold it open, his watchful eyes accessing me. The fear I see brimming in his dark gaze has my insides churning. With his lips pinched tightly he gives a hard shake of his head.

"If you get caught do you have any idea what he'll do to you?" he questions through clenched teeth.

As the elevator makes a banging noise, the doors trying to slam shut, I stand there in shock, hardly able to believe what I'm hearing. The handler is worried about me—about my safety—and more importantly he's not going to turn me in. I can only be grateful that it's Mario who found me and not Lawrence. I shiver just from thinking about that outcome, because I know I wouldn't be so lucky.

"How did you know where I was?" I ask carefully, maintaining a safe distance between us, my body still tensed and ready for combat. My wolf is still cautious, unsure, and reluctant to trust anyone in this prison.

"It was your turn to go up for the obstacle course and I couldn't find you. Then when I saw the two alphas fighting, and noticed you were missing, I put two and two together."

I frown, still not convinced. "And that led you here?"

"No, Mica told me."

I lower my head briefly and frown. "So Mica turned me in," I say under my breath, but I know better than to be angry at the aging housekeeper. After all, I wouldn't want her to risk her life for mine. In fact, I wouldn't want anyone to die because of me. That thought has me remembering Jace and Clover and my stomach twists.

Mario's head swishes from side to side, his long black ponytail flickering along his back. "You've got it wrong, Pride.

If she turned you in, it would have been Lawrence here fetching you, not me."

My heart misses a beat and my eyes come up to meet his. "Oh," I say quietly, and the implication that both Mario and Mica are in my corner fills me with relief.

He gestures with a nod for me to climb into the elevator with him. "Come on. We need to get out of here before anyone notices that we're gone."

I nod and hurry inside. When I move to the back corner, cool air from the venting system spills over me, but the only scents I catch in the breeze are Mario's.

Pressing my back to the wall, I fold my hands across my chest and stare at Mario's back as he jabs the button. When the elevator begins to move, he turns to me. His dark eyes narrow as they search my face for answers.

"What were you doing down here?"

I look at him long and hard and consider the handler's loyalties as I deliberate my next words. Is he really on my side, or is this a way for the master to figure out what I was doing in his chambers? But when I see real warmth and worry lingering in the depths of his worn and tired eyes, it does something to my insides and tells me what I need to know.

I can trust him.

I slowly open my hand to reveal the key sitting in the center of my palm, and Mario sucks in a sharp breath, his eyes widening as the overhead light glints off the shiny metal.

"Do you have any idea what you're doing?" His voice is low and grave, but I don't let it shatter my focus. I can't.

"Yes," I say with quiet certainty.

"Really, so you know what's waiting for you on the outside? Or even on the inside?" When I don't answer he makes a noise in his throat and I can't help but think he sounds like a wounded animal. "So you think you can just open your cage and walk out of here?"

"Not quite."

As the elevator slowly carries us I think of my army, the panthers, the gang waging war against the master.

"Pride—"

I cut him off and ask, "Why do you put up with what he does to you?" I pause to rake my hands over my thin, half-dressed body. "To us?"

He glares at me. His eyes turn hard and there is real anger in his tone when he says, "You don't know anything, little girl."

His words feel like a sharp slap and my head jerks back with a start, but I realize my accusing words have touched on a sore spot and I wonder exactly what it is.

"I know if we all work together we can change this. We can shift the balance of power inside this household and take over," I rush out, desperate to convince him.

"Did you ever stop to think about his connections on the outside, and what could happen to our families?"

Families?

I study him, and when I see equal measures of anger and concern pass over his dark eyes, my heart sinks, because I know. I know he's right. I never once stopped to take his situation or his family's into consideration.

"He's threatening your family?" I ask quietly and think about Mica, Miss Kara, and all the others who are in the same situation.

He nods and rakes shaky hands through his dark hair and I'm not sure what suddenly compels him to open up to me, but I do understand he's sharing something very personal when he continues, "I came here looking for a better life. Once I found it I was going to send for my family." His face softens and I see a slight smile when he say, "I have a little girl. She's about the same age as you and I wanted to offer her more."

Then, as quickly as it appeared, the softness in his voice disappears. His profile hardens and his head drops, his eyes go vacant as he stares at the cold metal floor beneath us. "But what I found here instead has done the opposite, and now my entire family is in danger." He stabs his thumb into his chest. "Because of me." He turns worried eyes my way. "He knows who they are, Pride. He knows where my wife lives. Where my kids go to school."

Tense silence hovers between us for a long time, then he holds his hands out, palms up. "Their future is in my hands. If I make one wrong move..."

"I'm going to kill him," I say.

His gaze flies to mine. "Things aren't that easy, Pride. You're still young and you really don't know the ways of the world."

"You're wrong, you know. Your family's future isn't in your hands. It's in the master's and it will stay that way unless we do something about it. If we kill him, your family won't be in danger, and then their future really will be in your hands and you can go get them."

"I'm not an assassin," he whispers.

"I am."

He doesn't speak. Instead he just stares at me, then he asks in a low, cautious voice, "Do you really think you can do it?"

I nod.

"How?"

Before I can answer the elevator comes to a halt and Mario returns to handler mode as the doors slide open. He steps off first and I'm about to follow, but when his footsteps still and his body goes stiff, I don't need to exit the elevator to know who's waiting for me in the hallway.

Acting purely on instinct, I quickly shove the key into my braid to hide it, and step into the narrow hallway. I harden myself and prepare for the worst, knowing I can't break cover.

I keep my expression blank, my eyes hard as I move in beside Mario, showing my obedience.

"Well, well, what do we have here?" the master asks, his shrewd glance going from Mario to me back to Mario again.

I don't want to get the handler in trouble, so I open my mouth to speak, even though I have no idea what I'm about to say, but Mario comes to my rescue and speaks first.

"She wanted to speak with you. She said it was urgent and I thought you were in your downstairs chambers, so I brought her to you."

The master rolls on his feet and juts his chin out as he considers this information. Then after a long agonizing minute he turns to me. "Is that so, Pride?"

I nod quickly, my brain scrambling to catch up. Then I realize that not only has Mario given me the perfect opportunity to prove my loyalties, he's also given me a rare opportunity to gather information. I have to clear my head and struggle to think straight, because I can't screw this up. I just can't. I have to give the master enough information to appease him, but I can't let him figure out how much I know.

"When I was in the courtyard today," I begin, and work to make it look like my concerns are for the master.

"Go on," he prompts.

"There was a strange new smell in the air."

I pause and wait to see if the master is going to react, but when he just continues to stand there, hovering over me like a silver bullet, I continue. "It was rank, like a cat."

He waves his hand. "We're in a vineyard, Pride. There are always stray cats about."

I open my eyes wide to accentuate the importance of what I'm saying. "This was different."

"Different how?"

"The scent taunted my wolf. She gets the sense that whatever is out there is a danger. To all of us."

"Is that right," he says, his eyes narrowing as if to figure out how much I know. "How so?"

I watch him carefully and that's when I hear it—the increased flow of his blood, the elevation of his heart rate, and the rapid jump in his pulse.

He knows what's out there. He knows what we're up against. And if he's this afraid, we're all in trouble.

As my wolf howls and feeds off his fear, I wonder who is commanding these panthers and what they'll do to the master if they get hold of him.

What will they do to the wolves once we escape?

"If something is out there threatening us, we're all going to have to work together to destroy it," I say, hoping he'll tell me exactly what we're up against but knowing better than to come right out and ask.

"So this is the reason you wanted to see me? To warn me that something is out there."

I nod.

"And to think that just yesterday you tried to attack me because I wanted to breed you." He gives a cruel smirk. "Such conflicting behavior does make me question whether you're working with me, or working against me."

"With you," I say and keep the urgency from my voice when I add, "Why would I have come here to warn you about the dangers on the outside."

"Why indeed?"

"Just because I don't want to breed doesn't mean I'm not loyal and I came to tell you because I don't want anything to happen to you."

"Don't worry, Pride," he says, letting me know the subject

is closed for discussion. And while I'm walking away without having gained much information at least I'm able to walk away from this, because I know this situation could have gone down a whole lot worse for me.

"I have everything under control." He makes a noise in his throat and takes a step closer to me. "If you really want to prove you're loyal then you won't put up a fight when I breed you in five days."

I stare at him and it suddenly occurs to me that he's stalling. Why would he wait for the full moon? I know it's when Stone is at his strongest and when I'm most fertile, but my instincts tell me he's putting off the mating for another reason. He needs something else from me.

"I won't put up a fight," I assure him. And I won't, simply because I plan on being gone from this prison long before then.

His smile is crooked when he turns to Mario, dismissing me like I'm yesterday's news. "Take her to her cell." Dark eyes move to mine when he says, "I'll see you in the courtyard tomorrow, Pride. It should be an interesting day."

Everything in his cruel gaze tells me he has something planned, something I'm not going to like.

Mario grips my arm, and when he gives it a tug to set me into motion, my ponytail swishes against my neck. My heart goes into my throat when I feel the key dislodges, the cold metal scraping over my nape. I suck in a sharp breath and hold it, just waiting for the ball to drop, or in this case, the key to slip free and clang on the cement floor.

We move past the master, and he stands there watching, his arms folded across his chest. I walk slowly, fearing he's going to see the key, to know what I've done.

Once Mario opens the door leading to the kitchen, I let the air out of my lungs, and inconspicuously run my hands along the length of my hair to slide the key into my palm before it falls.

I'm about to breathe a sigh of relief, but turn in time to see the master's savage smile before the thick metal door clicks shut behind us.

His smirk fills me with fear.

What does he have planned for the courtyard tomorrow?

10

A n uncomfortable silence falls over us as Mario leads me back to the cellar. His expression is bored as we pass by the master's staff but I can see the tension in his posture.

We reach the long staircase leading to my own personal dungeon and I descent the step slowly, prolonging the inevitable as my wolf howls desperately inside me. Our plan might have been to get in and out as quickly as possible and after promising her only one night of solitary confinements, it's slowly killing her to be back in the dank basement.

Forcing my legs to carry me into my cage, a cold chill falls over me as I enter but I embrace the discomfort. Once inside, I quiet my wolf and turn to face Mario, my expression questioning.

Does he know what the master has planned?

I search his eyes for answers, looking for something, anything to let me know what I'm going to be up against tomorrow. But from the strained look on his face, combined with the fatigue in his eyes, I can tell he's as in the dark as I am. Only the master knows what tomorrow will bring.

With that he closes the door gently and my heart beats faster as he secures my lock. Then his eyes meet mine, and he isn't even trying to mask the worry I see there.

"Do you have a plan?" he questions in whispered words.

"I'm working on it," I assure him, thankful that Sandy is still in the courtyard and we can talk privately.

He stands there for a long time, his forehead braced against the cage, then he lifts his head and the pain I see on his face presses against my heart. "I'm sorry, Pride."

"Don't," I say quickly, holding my hands up to stop him because I'm suddenly not sure I can deal with his pain or his emotions. Mine are in enough turmoil as it is.

But he doesn't stop. Instead he says, "I'm sorry I wasn't strong enough to stop him from doing this to you."

His fingers slip through my metal bars and when his hands tighten on them, I close my small palm over them.

"Please," I say, tears stinging my eyes. "This isn't your fault. You had a family to worry about. I understand that now."

He gives me a small grateful smile that doesn't reach his eyes when he whispers, "I don't want anything to happen to you."

I push the words past the lump in my throat. "I'll be fine."

After a long moment he breaks the quiet, gives a slow sure nod of his head and says, "If anyone can pull this off, Pride, it's you."

As his words ring in my head—words I once heard before from Clover before I bolted three weeks ago—it does something to me. Without conscious thought my hand fists over my heart. Even though Clover is gone, I know she's still with me, here in my heart, urging me to do the right thing. It was her confidence in my abilities that helped me escape the first time and the faith both she and Mario have in me will help me do what needs to be done a second time. I'm sure of it.

"Just be careful, okay?"

I nod but a bang at the top of the stairs has us both stiffening. Mario steps back. His back goes straight and his face hardens, then after returning to handler mode he twists and takes the stairs two at a time. A moment later I listen to the door slip shut, and the deadbolt slide home.

With chaos erupting inside me, I push down my emotions and turn to find bread and bacon wrapped in a small napkin. My stomach takes that moment to grumble, but before I dive into it and devour it like a starved dog, I hurry to the corner of my cot, lift it slightly, and gingerly place the key underneath. I don't dare try it on the lock just yet, not when anyone could come sauntering down the stairs and catch me. No, I'll have to wait until after dark, when the house is quiet and my bunkmate is asleep.

Once the key is hidden, I lower myself onto my cot. As I carefully peel open the napkin, I wonder who could have delivered this food to me. If I didn't know better I'd think I had my own little guardian angel. But I do know better. With the exception of a few, in this place it's pretty much every wolf for himself.

I breathe deep to see if I can catch any unfamiliar scents lingering in the air but when I find none I peer into Sandy's empty cage. Not that I think she'd share her victor's winnings with me, anyway.

I don't spend too much time thinking about who gifted me with this much needed nourishment, not with the way my belly is growling loudly. I take a bite and force myself to chew slowly, otherwise I know my empty stomach will rebel. The dry bread lodges in my throat, and without water I have to work extra hard to swallow it down.

Once I'm finished I lay on my cot, and soon Sandy returns. She comes bounding down the steps like an exuberant puppy, and after Lawrence deposits her in her cell, she crawls into her bed without saying a word to me. I note the curious way she's watching me, like she suspects I'm up to something.

Keeping my pulse steady and the blood flowing slowly through my vines to avoid raising her suspicions I turn from her, and use that time to think about my next move. But as I stare at the ventilation system overhead and think about the twists and turns I'll have to take to make my way around the upstairs, I wonder about my father's scent. Will I pick up on it again? If I catch a whiff, do I dare follow it? Will it lead me to answers? Or will it lead me to danger?

My heart pounds at that thought and my restless wolf, anxious to break free from her cell, howls for me to make my move. As impatience thrums through her I try to soothe her, to remind her that we can't ever act on impulse again. The noises ringing out upstairs are a sign that the household is still awake and we need to exercise both caution and restraint.

I close my eyes to rest them and a long time later, when I finally hear the upstairs settle, I turn to Sandy to find her breathing softly, a good indication that she's fallen asleep. I wait a moment longer just to be sure then ease myself from my cot. I drop to my knees, suck in air and quietly lift the corner of my cot. Even though I know it has to be there, I still breathe a sigh of relief when my gaze lands on the shiny new key.

I wrap my palm around it and hold it tight while I stuff my pillow under my ratty blanket to make it look like I'm still in bed asleep. Stepping back, I observe my handiwork. It's not convincing by any means, but it's the best I can do with limited supplies. With that I tip-toe to my cage door and as I mentally rehearse my plan, I can hardly believe what I'm about to do.

Quieting my heartbeat, I use slow, careful movements and

slip my small shaky hands through the narrow bars until the key is aligned with the lock. Despite the cold room, beads of moisture pool on my forehead, and I use my arm to wipe them away. I push the key in and almost howl with joy when it easily slips inside the keyhole, a perfect match.

I hold still for a minute and my ears twitch, half expecting the master to come barreling down the stairs because I've set off some sort of alarm. When nothing happens, and knowing I can't afford any distractions—anything that can rattle my hard earned focus—I return my full attention to the lock.

I give the key a quick twist and cringe when the bolt makes a loud clicking sound. Sandy rolls in her cot, the coils squeaking beneath her tiny frame. I hold my breath and remain still and the joints in my neck crack slightly as I angle my head to see her, to assure myself the sound hasn't dragged her from her slumber. When I find her eyes shut and her breathing slow and steady, I relax slightly and take a moment to regroup.

I take three deep breaths, then after getting myself under control I work quickly, pull the cage door open just enough to slip out, then I secure it shut behind me. I drop to the floor and hide the key between the cement pad and the bottom metal rail of my cell before I stand back up. Pushing myself further into the shadows, I brush the dirt from my hands and look overhead.

In the darkened room my eyes follow the path of the ventilation ducts and I somehow have to find the route that will lead me to Gem. But the first thing I need to do is get up high so I can reach it.

I move back to my cage, grip the metal bars and pull myself upward until I'm on the top of my cage. I rise up and stand on the long, narrow rungs. Spreading my arms to balance myself, I slowly put one foot in front of the other, my toes curling around the cold metal. I walk steadily, shoulders back and head held high, like Miss Kara taught me, until I'm directly beneath the ventilation duct. Without making a sound, I grip the jagged edge and with every ounce of strength I possess, I pull myself inside.

Once I'm into the darkened tunnel, I take a moment to breathe and try not to let myself get overwhelmed by the tight space as I gather my bearings.

I widen my arms and legs, bracing my palms and feet on the metal duct so I can shimmy upward. The tubing feels icy and slippery against my bare soles and it takes all my strength and determination to climb up. Once I reach the main level of the mansion, I take a moment to position myself, and work to settle my racing heart as I try to figure out where I am.

I push my hair from my face, wishing I'd kept it tied up. That's when I see a light up ahead, filtering into the ventilations system from a downstairs floor grate. I begin to crawl on my hands and knees toward it.

Every now and then the metal tubing makes a groaning sound beneath my light weight, and it forces me to stop and listen, making this mission that much harder, that much longer.

When I finally reach the plastic grate, I peer down and see the long hallway leading to the master's office. That's the last place I want to go—I have no doubt that he's in there planning and strategizing some brutal event for tomorrow. That thought has me hurrying onward. Even though I have no idea what cruelties he has in store, everything in my gut warns that it's meant for me.

As a cold shiver moves through my veins it elicits a quake from deep within, forcing me to use extra caution when climbing over the grate. Once I've cleared it, I exhale a breath I didn't realize I'd been holding and continue my forward trek.

When my duct comes to an abrupt end, only to meet up

with another channel running perpendicular to it, I consider my next move. Knowing I need to go east, I slide into the tunnel to my right, hoping it's the path that will lead me to Gem.

I crawl along the thin metal tubing, thankful for my size and my ability to move about the confined space swiftly and quietly. I stop every now and then to breathe deep in an attempt to capture Gem's scent. Off in the distance I hear noises and catch faint traces of conversation throughout the household. Senses finely tuned, I listen for anything that can help me, or pinpoint my exact location.

As I continue forward my mind takes that time to give further consideration to what Stone told me in the courtyard —that not all wolves want or can be saved. But I know that everyone, including wild animals, have a will to live and somehow I have to make them understand that what they're doing here isn't living.

It's simply surviving.

Everything about this abnormal situation goes against our primal nature, and no matter what, I have to convince them to turn their backs on all they've ever known and trust in me, because the truth of the matter is, I'm responsible for enough death as it is, and won't stand for any more.

Up ahead I see another grate, the soft white rays of light filter into the darkened tunnel and provide a pathway. I hurry to it in an effort to gather my bearings. I hover over the grate and peer through the plastic slats. While I'm not familiar with this wing of the estate, I sense that I'm getting close. I go deeper into the mansion and worry gnaws at me when I realize just how long this is taking. I work to memorize each twist and turn so I'll know how to find my way back. I can only hope I make it to my cot before Sandy wakes up.

As I approach another vent, I stop and breathe deep. That's when I catch Gem's distinctive scent.

My heart leaps and like a bloodhound on the hunt I pull in the scent and follow Gem's fragrance until I come to another grate. I look through it, and my pulse leaps when I spot what looks like a bedroom. A dim lamp casts shadows over the room and there is an eerie stillness, an unnatural silence that has the hairs on my nape rising.

I shift my focus and that's when I spot Gem in a small cage at the foot of a king sized bed. Her clothes are ripped, her long blood-crusted hair is matted to her head, and she doesn't appear to be breathing. I feel a moment of panic, but then I calm myself and listen closely. When I catch the faint sound of her blood moving through her veins, I know she's still alive.

Both relief and anger rushes through me. While I'm relieved to find her alive and breathing, it infuriates me that the master has kept her locked away from the others and is allowing her to remain in such a disheveled state.

And here I thought I couldn't hate him any more than I already do.

I want to call out to her, but I don't dare. I poke my hands through the grate and twist it until I'm able to dislodge it. When it pops from the wall with a loud snap, I turn my body until I'm lying on my stomach, push my legs through the tight opening and drop to the ground.

My feet land softly and I widen my stance to brace myself, expecting an attack. When none comes, I quickly assess the situation, dart across the carpeted floor, and sink to my knees in front of Gem's cage.

My heart clenches when I see the ragged state she's in. I reach inside and smooth my hand over her hair as I speak in whispered words, not wanting to startle her.

"Gem, you need to wake up."

Her dark lashes fling open and at first my heart seizes because her beautiful green eyes, eyes that once resembled precious gemstones, have lost their luster. They look blank, empty. Lost. Which begs the question, has the master broken her?

I keep my voice low but firm. "Gem, it's me, Pride," I say with forcefulness, hoping to snap her out of her stupor.

She blinks once, twice, then her eyes widened with recognition. "Pride," she whispers, before glancing past my shoulder. I follow her eyes and my body tenses as I look behind me, half expecting to find someone standing there.

Gem squirrels backward until she's pressed against the far end of her cage. Her guard goes up and she hugs her knees to her chest in a defensive reaction. Dread takes hold of me and as her throat makes an agonized sound, I fear if I don't get her out of here soon, I'll lose her to the dark side, like Sandy.

"Shhh," I whisper and put my finger to her lips.

"You shouldn't be in here. It's dangerous."

"Has he hurt you?"

She nods but says, "I'll be okay."

"I promise I'll get you out of here," I say, wanting her to understand that she's going to be okay before I begin to press for information.

She nods and loosens her hold on her knees. "Okay," she says without question and the amount of trust she's willing to place in me doesn't go unnoticed.

Without preamble I get right to the point. "I need to know everything you know."

She nods again.

I flick my head toward the window. "What happened out there? Tell me exactly how things went down."

Dark fear moves over her face and her look is distant and distracted and I can tell she's reliving horrible memories.

"Gem," I say again and reach though the cage to place my hand on her shoulder in an attempt to bring her focus back around to me. Her skin is hot, sticky, like she's running some sort of fever. Since werewolves don't get sick, I can't help but think the master has done something to her. I think back to the poison the officers injected into me when I was on the run, and remember how it made me feel.

Has the master injected her with something as well?

"Where is your pack?" I rush out, worry prompting me to push harder for information. "What happen to them?"

I see a new paleness in her face, a tension in her posture I've never seen before and her chest heaves when she says. "We were all positioned, waiting for the cannon to sound at noon so we could take out the handlers..." Her voice falls off and her brow furrows.

"But that didn't happen," I remind her. "What did?"

"It was broad daylight." She gives a slow shake of her head and her voice sounds strangled when she continues. "And we didn't even see them coming."

"Didn't see who coming?" I question, determined to get to the bottom of matters.

"Not who. *What* would be more accurate." Her hand catches hold of mine and a hot shiver rushes through my blood.

Determined to get the details from her I question, "Okay, what then?"

She exhales a shallow breath. "You're not going to believe me." Her brows collide and she gives a slow, perplexed shake of her head. "Honestly, I'm not even sure if I believe it. Maybe this fever is making me delirious."

I go back on my heels and give her hand a comforting squeeze to let her know she's not delirious. "Let me guess. You were attacked by shape-shifting panthers."

Surprise registers on her face and her eyes go wide. "How did you know?"

"I saw them on the monitors and when I mentioned it to Logan, he explained what they were."

"We've always been taught that other shifters existed, but I'd never seen anything like them before. They were long, black, sleek, and vicious."

"Did they..." My hands fall away as I stop speaking. I struggle to figure out how to push the next question past my lips, but I can tell she already knows what it is I'm trying to ask.

"No, they ran, and then the panthers took chase. Wolves are fast, but cats are fast, too."

"Do you think they caught them?"

"I don't know."

"How did you get away, Gem?"

She grips the cold bars of her small cage, her face close to mine. "I didn't."

I look at her, confused for a moment and then realize what she means. "No. I mean how did you get away from the panthers?"

"I didn't," she says again. "One trapped me. He was big, black and dangerous but what I remember most was his eyes. They were the deepest shade of gray I'd ever seen, but underneath all that feral hardness I saw something else."

"What was it?"

She looks down for a moment, her long lashes shadowing her emotions, then she whispers, "I think it was compassion. I think he felt sorry for me so he let me go."

For a moment my brain stalls. "He let you go?" I ask again, dumbfounded.

"Yes, and I used that opportunity to run for the front door of the mansion."

I frown and watch her stretch her legs out in front of herself. Even inside the small cage her movements are calculated and graceful, a reminder that while her name says it all —that she's vibrant and bubbly—in wolf form she's not only streamlined and fast, she can think on her feet.

"Why did you do that?" I ask. "Why didn't you run away?"

"I couldn't leave you in here thinking we'd abandoned you. Besides, I figured I'd be more help to you on the inside now that our plan failed."

Her response stuns me and I almost blurt out how wrong she is, how her capture has only slowed us down because we're unable to flee the courtyard until we figure out a way to free her or convince the master to place her in the cellar with the rest of us. But I can't bring myself to say those things, because I know it will only hurt her and she doesn't deserve that from me.

Instead I say, "We have to find your family, but we have to get out of here first."

"What's the new plan?" Her green eyes are wide and waiting, fully expecting me to have the solution.

But I don't. So I don't answer.

It does, however, occur to me that everyone is counting on me, putting their trust in me. I redirect the conversation and try to sound more sure of myself than I am. "Tell me, did you see or hear anyone else out there? Someone has to be controlling these shifters and we need to know what we're up against."

She goes quiet for a moment and her eyes narrow as they once again cast down in thought. Then a moment later her chin comes up with a start and I hear the quiver in her voice when she asks, "Do you think it could be the PTF?"

"No I don't," I say neglecting to tell her that whoever is harnessing panthers just might be more deadly than the PTF.

"Why?"

"Because they hunt all things that go bump in the night. They don't harness them."

"Then who?"

"That's what I need to find out."

Her eyes go serious as they track to the ventilation system

and I can almost hear her mind racing. "Tell me how you found me, Pride. How did you get out of your cell?"

"I found a key."

"Is it the master key?" she asks, a measure of hope back-lighting her vibrant green eyes.

My head comes back with a start. "Master key?" I ask. Is there really such a thing?

"Yes, the master keeps it secured to his belt. It's on this long stretchable elastic he keeps on his buckle."

I take a moment to reflect on that. I'm astute and aware, always taking note of everything around me and searching for a way out, which makes me wonder why I missed that very important detail. As I ponder that, Gem answers my unasked question.

"Since he's the one handling me, I've seen him use it. It opens all the doors." I see a new sparkle in her eyes and it gives me hope that she's going to be okay.

I catch hold of her hand again and my mouth drops as a new plan begins to formulate inside my brain. If I can get my hand on the master key then I can unlock all the cells and we can break out under the cover of darkness. Stone knows the code to the alarm system and can lead everyone to safety while I settle some unfinished business with the master.

But I can't forget that once we make it outside, we still have to face the beasts waiting for us beyond the perimeter. Except, I remind myself, they're not really after us. They're after the master. And I might be able to use that to my advantage.

"Does he ever take it off?"

"Yes, he's been keeping me close, leading me around with him and just last night when I was in his west wing office I saw him drop it into his desk drawer."

As I listen to Gem, I realize I'd been wrong in my thinking earlier. She is far more helpful on the inside that I ever could have imagined. It's because of her that I now have a new game plan.

I smile at her, finally understanding why Malcolm would bring her along. Not only is she smart, she has an incredible strength of character and is stronger than I ever realized.

"You're brilliant, Gem." Somewhere in the east wing an old grandfather clock chimes and I nearly jump out of my skin. I count the loud clangs as they ring out and realize how much time has passed.

Gem gives me a big toothy smile. "Why do you think they call me Gem?"

The truth is I thought it was because she was vibrant and sparkly, full of energy and life, not because she had a brilliant mind. And if it wasn't for her, I might never have fashioned a new plan and figured out my next step.

Which is to get into the master's office undetected, and get my hands on that master key.

11

I hate to turn my back on Gem and leave but under the circumstance I have no choice. Especially if I want to move about the vents undetected and get back before Sandy awakens.

After assuring Gem that I'll be back as soon as I can, I work to get my emotions under control so they don't end up getting the better of me. I have to think with clarity as I strategize the next stage of our escape. Moving about silently, I climb back into the shaft, knowing I can't make any mistakes as I secure the grate behind me and begin to retrace my steps back to my cell.

I take that time to consider what Gem told me and while I'd like to go straight to the master's office and have that key in my possession before we begin a new day, I know I've lost far too much time as it is.

I need to get back to my bunk before Sandy discovers I'm gone. My pulse races thinking about what she'd do with that knowledge, or how she'd use it against me and try to destroy everything we're working toward. My heart hurts for her, a bone deep ache that I'm sure I'll forever carry. I can only hope that someday she'll stop disliking me and see the master for what he really is.

As much as I hate to stay locked in my cage for another night—I'd really like to break out of this prison before I'm forced to face whatever it is the master has planned for the courtyard tomorrow—I have no choice but to sit tight and tame my wolf. While I'd like to let her off her leash, I know better than to hurry things along. Rushing only leads to mistakes and every move I make in this deadly game of life and death must be played with intelligence and strategy.

Once I'm back in my own room, I drop onto the top of my cage, bracing my feet on the metal bars as I regain my balance. Then I move with agility, without sound as I make my way to the edge of my cell. I roll onto my stomach and slide down the bar. After my feet hit the floor, I reach for the key, open my door and slip inside. I take a quick peek at Sandy to ensure she's still asleep before I lift the corner of my cot and place the key beneath for safe keeping.

By the time I settle myself into my bed, my heart is racing a million miles an hour and there is nothing I can do to settle my shuffling thoughts. The fact that freedom for all is so close that I can almost taste it, not to mention the huge spike in my adrenaline, makes it difficult for me to unwind. But I force my eyes shut and will my body and brain to relax.

When I open my eyes again, I know a new day is upon me. I turn to find Sandy staring at me, shards of silver puncture the brown in her eyes as her wolf growls at me.

"Sandy," I say to her in a soft tone, needing most desperately for her to understand I'm on her side, but taking care not to give away my plan to early. "Everything is going to be okay."

When she doesn't respond, my eyes go to her stomach. For a brief moment I wonder about her pups, and wonder if Stone will be a good father. It saddens me to think that he had no father of his own, no positive role model in his life. My thoughts stray to Logan's father and what he taught the young alpha before he died: hunting, fishing, nurturing—things Stone never had the chance to learn from a father figure. But thinking about fathers has me thinking of my own.

I roll onto my back and stare at the ventilation system. While it was only two days ago that I picked up on my papa's scent, it feels like a lifetime has passed, and has me questioning what's real and what isn't. Maybe he's not really here in the mansion, at all. Maybe he hadn't come to me in person, or in a dream. Then again, maybe that's just wishful thinking.

It's not that I don't hope he's alive. I do. But if he is alive and he's here asking me to forgive him, then it means he's done something he needs forgiveness for.

And since I know nothing about forgiveness…

When I hear the lock upstairs my stomach sours. I remember the master's cruel smile and that he has something special planned for me today.

Mario descends the stairs slowly and my senses go on high alert. I listen to his blood flow through his veins, slow and steady, but underneath that superficial shell I can smell his anxiety. From Sandy's agitated state, it's clear her wolf has picked up on it too.

I track his movements and I instantly realize he's having a hard time meeting my gaze, which speaks volumes.

He knows my fate.

My pulse leaps and I jump from my cot. I want to ask him what he knows but the words catch in my throat because I don't dare question him in front of Sandy.

Moving quickly and efficiently like he does every other morning, he goes through the monotonous routine of unlocking us from our cages and fitting us with those heavy, uncomfortable collars. Then he hooks a chain to the restraining bands around our necks and herds us through the kitchen until we're both outside.

I pull in the scents around me, wondering if the panthers are still in the vicinity. Have they captured Logan's family or worse...

Once we're in the courtyard numerous wolves move around me, sizing me up and pulling in my scent. I swallow and wish there was a way for me to reach out to them. I wish I could make them understand that if we all worked together we could outman the master. But the despair I see in their eyes lets me know they're broken and loyal.

Mario proceeds to unhook Sandy. As she sheds her nightgown and shifts I use that time to search for Logan and Stone. I try not to show a reaction when I spot them in the distance, both keeping a wary eye on each other and the other eye on me.

Looking for a distraction, I angle my head in time to see Sandy run her paws through the dewy grass and turn her muzzle to the sky to drink in the warm morning rays. As I watch her, and remember that she has babies growing inside of her, it renews my vow to get out of here, but in the meantime I know I need to win my race today. Winning means I can give her extra food.

Determination courses through me when I turn back to Mario. His gaze meets mine as he removes my collar, and I see real worry in his eyes. But his voice is calm when he says, "The master pitted you against Logan today."

Logan? I consider that for a moment and wonder why the master would pit me against a powerful alpha; one who no other wolf in the courtyard—except maybe Stone—could possible beat.

Is he simply setting me up for failure?

"So this is what he had planned?" I ask, thinking it can't be this easy. Nothing is ever this easy.

What am I missing?

As I stress about that, I realize there is no way I can win today's obstacle course, not if I'm pitted against Logan, which means I won't be able to share any of my victor's winnings with Sandy. But that isn't going to stop me from finding another way to get her the nourishment she needs. Perhaps my guardian angel will deliver bread and bacon once again, and I can offer it to her.

"You're both up first." I can tell by the look on his face he's trying to warn me about something. I look past his shoulders to take in the course. Is there some fatal flaw he fears I'm going to miss?

When I don't see anything unusual I turn back to Mario. "What is he hoping to accomplish by this?" I ask in whispered words.

Mario's eyes go dark and his voice hardens when he says, "You tell me."

I take a moment to puzzle it out, then I make a noise, a half grunt, half growl as understanding hits like a fatal blow. "He knows," I whisper through grit teeth. "He's testing us."

"He *thinks* he knows."

I glance around frantically, searching for my mate. I need to talk to him, to warn him. He can't let me win. But how can I convince an alpha to go against nature and let his mate go hungry while he gorges himself on fresh food?

Stepping away from Mario, I move toward the wall, pull off my nightgown and neatly fold it. I allow my body to shift, then sit back on my haunches and proceed to groom myself as I search for Logan, wanting to make a private connection. That's when I see him taking his position at the obstacle course.

Mario steps back up to me and leads me toward Logan. I browse around and take in all the eyes staring at us. From my peripheral I spot the master coming from his private entrance. Of course he wouldn't miss this.

"*Logan,*" I hurry out when I move in beside him. "*This is a test and you can't let me win.*"

He looks at me and his muscles bunch as his shrewd eyes rake over my light fur. Now that I'm back inside the compound and half starved, my coat is thinning, lacking in luster. When I glimpse the quiet reflective side of him, a side that reminds me he's just a boy and I'm just a girl, I instinctively go back on my haunches and try to groom myself. I preen myself casually not wanting Logan to notice how matted and mussed I look.

He turns his head from me and sets his jaw like the discussion is over. "*You need to eat.*"

"*I did eat. Someone left food for me last night.*"

"*Who—*" he begins like he doesn't believe me.

I steel myself. "*I don't know.*"

"*Pride—*"

The worry I hear in his voice tugs at my heart. Hot emotions erupt inside me and all I want to do is wrap my arms around him and hold him tight, sharing bonds and intimacies like we used to do when we were in the woods. I draw a sharp breath in and fight the natural inclination to comfort my mate, to accept his comfort in return.

I know Logan is a giver not a taker, a boy who would go against his own best interests for his mate. And while I know he would die for me, he would never allow me to die for him.

"*I have a new plan. Logan,*" I rush out before I do something stupid, like act on my feelings and brush my muzzle over his. "*And if we want it to work, then you have to win this race and show no empathy toward me.*"

He gives a savage shake of his head, his pewter eyes enraged as he digs his talons into the ground. His voice is deep, gravelly. "*You know I can't do that.*"

I feel a moment of panic when I see the guard move toward us with the starter gun. Logan is a protective alpha, and letting his mate suffer goes against everything he believes in, everything he's been taught. So when I say the next words it's for his own good. For the greater good.

Steadying myself, I jerk my head toward Stone and keep my voice deadpan when I say, "*Maybe you should take a lesson from him. He'd never mess this up.*"

My words are cold, cruel, delivering such a brutal punch Logan's head comes up with a start, and even though I don't want to hurt him, from the intense look in his pewter eyes, I know my words have cut deep.

I take a deep breath to center myself and search for a glimmer of understanding as I angle my head. "*He's watching and waiting for one of us to give. If we do, it gives him bargaining power and we can't allow that to happen.*"

"*What's your plan,*" he says without looking at me.

"*I found Gem, Logan. I found her,*" I hurry out and I can feel a sense of relief move through him as the guard takes his position. "*She told me where I can find the master key. I'm going to get it tonight, then we're all getting out of here.*"

He turns to me, his eyes are troubled yet trusting, but before I can tell him anymore, the starter gun sounds. Tuning out those around me, I hit the ground running and when I notice he's keeping pace, my insides twist with worry.

But he's my mate I remind myself, one of the smartest and strongest wolves I know, which means he'll do what I ask of him, even though it goes against everything he believes in and he'll undoubtedly hate himself for it. Warmth moves through me as I think about everything he's done for me so far. Logan is an amazing boy, a remarkable mate, a wolf who has so much respect for life and nature and I couldn't be more proud of him.

His gaze flickers to mine and when his warm familiar

scent seeps under my fur and wraps around me like a protective blanket, I spot something beneath the gray storm
brewing in the depth of his eyes. Something warm and understanding and I know in an instant he's read my thoughts.

Feeling almost embarrassed, I turn back to the obstacle
course and using every ounce of strength I possess I scale the
wall, clamp down hard on the thick rope and swing across the
soupy mud pit taunting me from below. Just because he's the
alpha, it doesn't mean I'm going to make this easy for him.
I'm certainly not a girl to go down without a fight and I plan
to challenge him until the end.

We run as equals, but soon Logan takes the lead, his hard
streamlined body and long powerful legs pushing past mine as
I slow on the hurdles. When the cannon sounds in the
distance I think about the master, my failed plan. Even
though he's a human, he's fully aware of canine behavior and
he knows full well that an alpha would never let his mate go
on scraps. But I wonder if this win is enough to convince him
that we don't have a bond.

That we didn't mate in Olympic Park.

In no time at all Logan finishes the course, but I come in
close behind him. We pace uneasily and take that time to
regulate our breathing. When I see Mario coming with our
clothes, I take that time to shift back to human.

Mario steps up to Logan first and slaps a collar around his
neck. Then without so much as sparing me a look, he leads
him toward the kitchen so he can dine of the finest food.

Before Logan enters the house, he slants his head and
turns piercing blue eyes on me. The distress I see on his face
showcases his every emotion and turns me inside out. I twist
away from him and meet Stone's glance. There I see eyes that
have witnessed so much carnage, so much bloodshed.

Eyes that have seen me give myself to another boy.

My heart clenches as my gaze flips back and forth

between the two and it dawns on me that while they're both alphas, they're a complete contradiction to each other.

Logan and Stone might be strong, powerful and fearless in the face of danger but they have completely different ways of exerting their dominance. One respects my strength and independence, the other wants to be that strength and independence. Perhaps it's because one was raised in captivity and one wasn't.

Either way, I'm not saying one way is right and the other is wrong. I'm just saying...

Actually, I don't know what I'm saying.

But I do know that Stone and I counted on each other for survival on the inside, Logan and I on the outside. What will happen between the three of us if we escape?

What will happen if we don't?

I turn my head and give it a mental shake, refusing to go down that path. I can only deal with one roadblock at a time and when I see the master closing the distance between us I know I need to pull myself together and focus my thoughts. Because right now the only thing I can think about is survival. But as he gets closer, my nape tingles because I sense a change in him. His face is hard. His eyes are dark. But there is a sense of satisfaction rolling through him that is impossible to miss.

What is happening?

Does he know about the missing key?

I usually only see him like this when he's sending us out on a hunt, or when he's about to pump a wolf with silver.

I know he's not about to send me out, which means...

When a sudden breeze comes out of nowhere and howls around me, a bad feeling moves into my stomach. I sense that I might very well be at the end of my journey.

I stand my ground and lift my chin up as he and Lawrence approach at the same time. The master's dark cruel eyes move over me, a slow careful assessment that makes my skin crawl, as Lawrence slaps a collar and chain around my neck.

"Hello, Pride."

I don't say anything. I can't. His large body dwarfs mine and I just glare up at him, trying not to choke on his foul cologne as it pollutes the air and stings my nose.

Dressed in his casual attire, my focus flickers to his jeans, and I feel a little jolt of hope when I don't see his master key. But will I ever get the chance to steal it, or will the master take this moment to make an example out of me. He folds his arms across his chest and rocks on his heels.

"There's been a change of plans."

My heart stalls as I wait for him to elaborate, everything in my gut warning me something very bad is about to go down.

He slowly angles his head to see me and I wonder what he's about to throw at me next. He's smiling but there is no humor in his eyes or softness in his words when he says, "You were right when you said I can't have two alphas in the court-yard, so I think I need to do something about it."

My stomach tightens and I feel bile pushing into my throat. I growl and in response Lawrence gives a hard yank on my chain to warn me.

"I need to restore the balance." The master turns away to look at Logan before he disappears inside. Then he scrubs his hand over his jaw before he turns back to me. "What I think I'll do is pit the two alphas against each other. A fight to the death."

As the full weight of his words him me, I want to scream. I want to protest.

I want to kill.

My heart seizes as I draw a savage breath. "No," I cry out, and acting purely on animal instincts I hurl myself at him, but the chain around my neck tightens and Lawrence jerks me back, his lips twisting in a hard smile. I wail as I land on the ground with a pounding thud.

"Oh don't worry, Pride. It won't be so bad."

I flip over and brace myself on my hands and knees, barely able to comprehend what he's saying. My nostrils flare, my lips curl back to expose sharp canines, and if I didn't have my collar on, I'd shift and make a clean kill right here and now. And not even the six guns pointed at me from above would be able to stop me before I ripped his throat out.

He looks at me like he's throwing me a bone when he says, "After all, it is female instinct to breed with the strongest male isn't it, Pride?"

Blind panic fills me as I work to digest his words. "What are you getting at?" I spit out and don't care what kind of abuse he's about to dole out for my behavior.

His back straightens and he levels me with a glare. "Whoever wins gets to claim you as his mate, of course."

12

I fight down a dark shudder but still can't shake the bone-deep cold turning my blood to ice as I pace restlessly around my cell. Impatience runs heavy in my veins, and only one thought keeps rattling around inside my brain: get the master key and free the wolves before Logan and Stone are forced to fight to the death.

I wring my hands together and frantically work to calm my thoughts. I have to clear my mind and keep my vision focused on my mission if I want to pull it off. Failure is not an option, otherwise tomorrow will end in bloodshed and I refuse to let that happen. I won't let anyone else die at the hands of the master because of me.

Once the upstairs has grown quiet and I'm sure Sandy is asleep in her bunk, I let myself out of my cage and climb back into the ventilation system. Moving with speed I retrace my steps to the master's office. I try to quiet my rapid heartbeat as I approach and valiantly struggle to keep my breathing regulated as panic threatens to overtake me.

Soon enough the scent of the master overwhelms my

senses and my blood curdles like spoiled milk. That's when I know I'm near. I crawl toward the shaft at the end of the tunnel, the one that will lead me directly to his office. When I see light filtering in the vents a hot wave of dread hits me. There is only one reason his light would be on.

He's inside.

With his presence putting a crimp in my plan, I slow my pace and slide along the duct until I can peer through the plastic slats. When I see the master sitting alone at his desk my wolf howls with pleasure, and that's when it suddenly dawns on me. This turn of events isn't a bad thing after all. Finding him inside alone provides me the perfect opportunity to let my wolf off her leash so she can crash through the wall, go for his throat, and end this once and for all.

Instincts sharpened, I can feel her pulling at me, clawing her way from my body. My nails elongate and my snout punches from my mouth, but when heavy footsteps herald the arrival of someone else, I crouch low, hush my blood hungry wolf and wait in hiding.

The master glances toward his door, and the heavy lines around his eyes fold as he smiles. And when he gestures with a wave, an indication for his visitor to have a seat, my heart goes into my throat and I clamp my hand over my mouth to keep myself from screaming.

I don't need to see his visitor to know who he is. His smell hits me like a hard fist to the gut and curls around my body like a deadly serpent. Fear rushes through me and my mind rebels, some small coherent part of my brain letting me know I was right all along—there really are things going on inside the mansion that I don't want to know—things I might not be able to handle.

Even with the turmoil shutting down my ability to think with any sort of clarity, it doesn't go unnoticed by me that the master is smiling, welcoming this visitor like they're old friends.

Waves of nausea flood my stomach and it takes every ounce of willpower I have not to vomit. Sweat breaks out on my body, despite the cool air rushing through the ducts and chilling my flesh.

I press my hands to my ears to still my racing mind, and as I block out the world and all its cruelties, Stone's words of warning pierce my thoughts. *"Run. It isn't safe for you here anymore."*

Is this what he was trying to protect me from?

Then my thoughts race a million miles a minute only to settle on Mario. I take a quick moment to recall the words he spoke to me in the elevator. *"Do you have any idea what's waiting for you on the outside? Or even on the inside?"*

All along I thought he was referring to the master, and never once stopped to consider that he was warning me about the man who disappeared from my life when I was just a pup, a man I once called father.

I brace my palms on the sides of the metal duct and take deep breaths as emotions ambush me, desperate to slow my chaotic thoughts so I can hear what they're saying. What they're planning.

I catch snippets of the conversation, and as the pieces of the puzzle known as my father come together to form a clear picture it becomes glaringly apparent who rules all the new wolves in the courtyard and how these two brutal men are creating a formidable army.

How could he have done this to his own kind?

His wife?

His daughter?

My wolf wails and my heart seizes. Then I hear them discussing Gem. The master informs my father that he's found the key to breaking her and come tomorrow morning she'll be under his full control.

As air evacuates my lungs, my blood thickens to a heavy sludge and I can't seem to push it through my veins. Feeling lightheaded I sink backward, emotionally battered and not quite sure how to deal with this turn of events.

I suck air and try to refuel my body with oxygen as I remember my father's parting words when he came to me in my cage just two days ago. *"Some things are worse than death."*

Finding out your father is a drug lord who's harboring wolves of his own and using them to assassinate others definitely ranks right up there in my books.

My head goes from left to right as I sort through this new information. I need to move. I need to run. I need to do something.

Just then my father stands, and I don't dare move, let alone breathe. He turns his back to the master and when his attention flickers to the duct, his eyes meeting mine, my heart goes into my throat and a gasp rips from my lungs.

He knows! He knows I'm here.

I squirrel backward and hold my breath. My pulse thrums in my throat as I wait for the silver to pierce, but when he leaves the master's office I don't hang around to find out if he's coming back. Instead, I turn, scurry through the ducts and hurry back toward my cage. Tears sting my eyes and blur my vision, but I continue to push forward, going left and right and getting myself all turned around as emotions tear me up inside.

I go deeper into the ducts and suddenly don't know where I am anymore. But what does it matter now? My plan has failed miserably. I press the heel of my hands to my eyes and realize I've never felt so alone before. So lost. So completely and utterly defeated. And I can't forget how many people are counting on me. How can I possibly tell them I failed, that I've let them all down?

As grief overwhelms me, my world feels like it's on the verge of collapsing. I sink backwards, my body and legs numb as I use the back of my hand to brush the moisture from my eyes, and that's when I hear a deep growl rumbling through the vents, rolling toward me like a huge, thunderous snowball. It instantly cuts through the chaos in my mind.

"*Stone*," I cry out, opening my thoughts as I frantically search for him.

"*Pride*," he returns and even though his voice is faint inside my head, I hear such emotion and turmoil in that one word that I know he knows.

He knows I found out the truth about my father.

"*Pride, where are you?*"

"*I don't know.*" I look around it the darkened duct. I sniff and say, "*I'm lost.*"

"*Reach out to me and follow the sound of my voice.*"

I do as he says, and soon my legs are moving again. I make my way though the vents guided only by instinct until I can feel his voice getting stronger and stronger inside my head.

When I reach his vent, I ease myself out, and land on the hard cement floor with a thud. Heart hammering, I take in his quarters and that's when I see his sleeping bunk mates, Cruz and Star.

Stone presses his fingers to his lips and gestures me closer. With my knees threatening to give, I sag against his cage and when he reaches through the bars and curls his arms around me, we both sink to the floor. A shiver wracks my body and he holds me tighter, offering me his warmth and protection.

We stay locked together for a long time, two lost wolves seeking comfort in the darkened cellar. I choke back tears and when I sniff I breathe in his scent. There's something so primal and raw about this alpha that it almost makes me feel safe.

"Stone," I begin, breaking the quiet, but then I close my mouth because no words need to be said between us.

Sensitive to my needs, Stone brushes the rough pad of his thumb over my cheek and the tenderness in his touch has me melting against him.

"Shh," he whispers and I sidle closer as his soft words fall over me like a comforting blanket.

Cradled in his arms, his warm familiar scent seeps under my skin and I know it's wrong to take comfort in his touch— which feels far more emotional than physical. Yet, as Stone adjusts his body and pulls me impossibly closer, I don't stop him. I don't even lecture myself on how wrong this is.

His hold tightens and my small frame crushes against his and while everything inside me is warning that I should run, that I should get as far away from this alpha as I possibly can, I let him wrap his arms around me, let him absorb my grief and fears. He's protective, caring and familiar and right now and I need that more than I need my next breath.

"You were trying to protect me," I finally say, tipping my head to look into his eyes.

He drags his fingers through my hair to tuck it behind my ear, then his eyes move over my face before dips his head and presses his mouth to my forehead. His warm breath washes over my flesh when he whispers, "I didn't want you to know."

I blink a fat tear from my eyes. "How long have you known?"

"Only recently."

I take a minute to process then say, "He reached out to me the other night." A shudder moves through me when I add, "Until tonight, I never knew if he was really here in the mansion or if he was simply a figment of my imagination." For a brief moment my mind goes to the bread and bacon left for me. I'm not sure why I'm thinking about that, or why it seems significant, but I suddenly have the sense that he left it for me. Honestly, if I had known, I never would have touched it. I'd rather starve than take anything from him.

Stone inches back, his brow furrows as he looks me over. "He came to you in your cage?"

I nod and Stone's face goes dark. "What did he want?"

I run over our conversation. "My forgiveness."

This seems to take Stone by surprise. "Your forgiveness. What is he asking you to forgive?"

"I...I guess for what he's done. Or maybe it's for something he's going to do. I don't know."

"I don't know either, Pride. I just don't know." He goes quiet and he brushes the rough pad of his thumb over my cheek.

I blink up at him. "What I don't understand is how he started working with our master. I know I was young and don't remember a whole lot but wasn't he a caged wolf like the rest of us?"

"Your father was a very powerful alpha. Maybe he was the one who had our master under control."

That thought catches me by surprise, but speaking of powerful alphas has me thinking about tomorrow. I swallow uneasily and when I say, "About tomorrow," I see a strain in his Stone's eyes when they settled on me.

"What about it?"

"Can you walk away?"

Anger sharpens his words and his muscles tighten, but he still doesn't pull away from me. "So you've made your choice then?"

"Stone," I hurry out. "I don't want anything to happen to you or Logan."

I see a flash of possessiveness in his eyes and a low growl

rumbles in his throat as his lips compress. "I'll be fine," he answers through grit teeth.

I work to keep myself from sounding frantic, knowing he won't be fine. In a struggle for power, Stone should never underestimate Logan, which makes it all that much more important for me to put a stop to this. "You don't have to do this." An ominous wave of heaviness falls over us and the air crackles with tension.

"Do you really think I'm going to walk away?" His nostrils flare and emotions thicken his voice. "And here I thought you knew me better than that."

"Can't you just be happy and settle down with Sandy?" I plead, trying to change tactics.

He gives me a perplexed frown and questions, "Sandy? Why would you think I'd want to settle down with Sandy?"

"Aren't you...?" My voice falls off as I reconsider the situation. "Didn't the master make you...?"

"Make me what?"

"Make you breed with Sandy," I finally choke out.

Understand dawns in his eyes, then it fades to disappointment. "You think I'd do that?"

"Only if you had no choice," I go on to explain, wanting him to know I understand. Sometimes we do what we have to do to survive.

Which begs the question, did I mate with Logan because it meant surviving? Or did I mate with him because I chose him?

Stone's face goes dark, thoughtful for a moment and he gives me a look I can't quite decipher. "When you first brought up her pregnancy in the courtyard I thought you were angry with me for not being able to stop it."

"That's why you were defensive?" I pause for a moment. "I thought it was because—"

"I'm not the father, Pride," he says, and I feel a strange

sense of relief rushing through me, then anger moves in to take its place, considering I shouldn't be worrying about such a thing when there is so much more at stake.

"Then who is?" I ask quietly.

"I don't know. You've seen all the new wolves in the court-yard. It could be any one of them."

Thinking about all the new wolves—animals under the control of my dear old dad—has me once again thinking of the master and what he wants Stone and Logan to do. A moment of silence falls between then I blurt out, "I don't want you to fight with Logan."

"You know I don't have a choice," he counters and the look on his face is almost frightening.

I briefly close my eyes in distress. "Yes, you do. You can walk away."

The muscles along his jaw ripple and his eyes are hard, unwavering when he says, "What if I don't want to, Pride? Have you ever stopped to think of that?"

"Stone," I say, and pound on his chest, the lump in my throat aching painfully.

A small frown forms on his forehead as he grips my fists and pulls them to his mouth. His warm lips press against my fingers to seal my protest and he just holds me like that for a long moment. Then, taking me by surprise, he lowers my hands and his lips move to mine. My breath catches in my throat at that first soft touch. His kiss is so gentle, so achingly tender and so needy it catches me off guard and has my entire body going weak.

Blindsided by his actions, my thoughts derail and a melee of emotions run through me. As Stone connects with me in a possessive way, a way only a mate should, it begins whittling away what little control I have. Then when I feel his hunger —dark, primal, needy—and hear a low growl in the depths of his throat my composure begins to slip. I tremble from head to toe and my hackles bristle, a physical reaction to Stone's alpha wolf.

As a storm broils inside me and my head begins to buzz, Stone inches away and severs the intimacy. He lets out a long-suffering sigh and I've never seen him look so tortured when he says, "It's getting late. You'd better get back before someone notices you're missing."

13

With Stone's familiar scent all over me, I carefully make my way back to my cage. After I finally find the vent leading to my quarters, I slip through the tight shaft, let myself into my den and hide the key before climbing into my cot.

My thoughts race a million miles an hour, trying to sort through everything that has happened tonight, from finding my traitorous father alive and learning he's a drug lord in cahoots with the master, to taking comfort in Stone's arms while my mate sits all alone in his cage prepared to fight to the death for me—the girl he chose above all others. And I can't forget about Gem, and what the master said about breaking her.

Guilt and fear eat at me and I shift restlessly on my tattered blankets, knowing I'm going I have a sleepless night ahead of me and feeling like I deserve one.

If my father is a traitor what does that make me? Will I eventually turn out like him? Turning my back on those I care about for my own selfish purposes?

Then again, maybe he never cared about me at all.

My heart clenches and I fight back the hot sting of tears. I toss in my bed and the worn springs groan as I think about tomorrow and what it will bring.

Will Stone walk away like I asked?

What will Logan do? After one look at me he'll surely know I found comfort in Stone's arms. Will he be the one to turn his back on me?

Unable to get comfortable I flip over on my mattress again, and I pound the dusty cot as a low torture moan crawls out of my throat.

I toss and turn for hours, until Lawrence finally comes for us. I climb from my cot, and with my body tired and my sleep deprived brain making me feel completely unstable and desperately emotional, not even the cold cement floor can pull me from my stupor.

Out in the courtyard I squint against the blinding sun and there is little I can do to shake the fuzz from my brain as I wait for Logan and Stone to appear. I push away from the crowd as Sandy is led to the obstacle course. Since I was unable to get food to her yesterday, I pray she wins the competition. She's pregnant, which means she get a daily allotment, but because she's so thin she needs the nourishment that comes with victory.

With one eye on Sandy and the other on the crowd I search for Logan and Stone. A long while later after Sandy finishes up her race and is led inside to eat because she's beaten her opponent, I see Logan moving past her as he enters the yard through the kitchen entrance, Lawrence standing behind him, gun in hand.

Logan looks hard and dangerous, but his guard slips a little when his eyes meet mine and my stomach revolts because I sense that he knows I've betrayed him. Guilt rushes through me and everything inside me reaches out to him, asking for forgiveness. But thinking about forgiveness has me thinking of my father and what he said to me. *"Sometimes we have to do what we have to do."*

Then I turn to see Stone closing in from behind, a powerful wolf on a mission. I swallow hard and wet my suddenly dry lips. When I do, I can taste my own fear as it saturates the warm air around me.

At the sight of the two moving toward the center of the yard, the other wolves all move back to give the two alphas room to fight. Clearly news of this deadly battle has spread through the underground quicker than a mutating virus. In no time at all cheers originate in the crowd, the restless wolves goading the two alphas on.

Soon animal instincts take over and Logan and Stone begin circling one another, both looking for a weakness that could give them an advantage.

I brace myself, and when a cold chill races through me, I fold my arms across my chest and hug my nightgown to my body, but the thin material does little to warm me. My eyes slip shut against the flood of emotion and heartache sets my chest on fire because I realize there is nothing I can do to stop this. Someone I care deeply about is going to die today.

Because of me.

As I stand there paralyzed with fear, I hear footsteps coming close. I don't need to turn to know it's the master. I can smell his excitement long before I see him. He stands beside me and I don't even acknowledge his presence until he speaks to me and what he says has both rage and relief unraveling inside my gut.

"There is a way you can stop this, Pride."

I angle my head slowly as my wolf clamors to break free and tear bone from flesh. His eyes glint knowingly and when our gazes clash in a battle of wills the master's face changes. As his smile vanishes his expression turns hard, cruel. Merciless. Intense eyes study me darkly and I know he's waiting for me to falter.

I snarl at him and it occurs to me that he's shrewd and cunning and has known all along how I feel about Logan and Stone. He's been toying with me. Playing me for a fool, because he knew he was eventually going to get what he wanted from me.

"What do you want me to do?"

"You already know," he answers.

He's right. I do know. I give a fierce shake of my head. "You can't ask me to do that."

"I can and I am."

I turn back in time to see Logan go for Stone's throat. When his canines puncture fur and flesh, hot blood shoots into the air, the scent filling my senses and causing a soft rumble to swell through the crowd.

I swallow, never having felt so scared, so out of control in my life and I know in an instant I can't do this anymore. I can't stand here and watch the two wolves I care about most tear each other to shreds. My heart races and mayhem erupts inside me as the brutal fight I'm forced to witness drains the good out of me.

I suddenly don't feel so tough anymore.

"Pride," the master says and the urgency I sense in him brings my attention back around to him. "If you want to save these two, then you'll tell me where to find Logan's pack."

My rattled brain registers the sound of snapping bones, followed by a painful howl and I'm no longer able to tell which wolf is winning, which wolf is dying. An unnatural black wave of despair grips me and I can feel the darkness inside me spreading onward and outward until my thoughts are a jumbled mess.

As a sick knot twists in my stomach I know in an instant I've reached the end. The master has won.

And it's that horrible, rancid scent of defeat curling around me and polluting the air that brings Logan's head swinging around to me. His pewter eyes glare at me like he knows I'm about to spill secrets, about to expose his entire family.

He gives a savage shake of his head, and the distraction allows Stone to gain the upper hand. Stone pounces and when Logan tumbles across the ground I can hear the air leaving his lungs in an agonized whoosh.

"Stop," I say frantically. "Don't do this." I turn to the master. "I'll tell you where his pack lives. I'll tell you where to find them. I'll tell you everything. Just stop this now."

He rolls on the balls of his feet and puts his hands into the pockets of his expensive suit, like he's in no hurry to end the fight.

"No, Pride. I think I'd rather you take me to them."

I open my mouth to protest but he cuts me off and snaps his fingers at Mario. "Take her to her cage and tell Kara to have her ready to leave at first light."

With that the master grips my chin, and turns my head from side to side to examine me. "Your father would have been proud of you, Pride."

"I don't have a father," I spit out and jerk my chin free. My blood pounds so hard in my ears I can barely think straight. I glance at the two wolves rolling around on the ground and bile pushes into my throat.

"You said you'd stop this," I remind him.

He grins and for a brief second I wonder if he's going to follow through with his promise, but then he snaps his fingers. Six gun shots crack the air, and the alphas separate. Lawrence stands back and tosses two collars at the wolves. I breathe a sigh of relief but it's short lived because when

Logan shifts back to his human form and looks at me with eyes full of disappointment and anger, my heart clenches and I know I've let him down.

I've let everyone down.

But what other choice do I have?

14

With my mind sorting things through, I keep my head down as I'm led back inside. I hate myself for my moment of weakness, hate that I let everyone down and while I might have saved Logan and Stone, I've put so many more wolves in danger.

As I leave the courtyard, I can't bring myself to look at my mate and while I can hear Stone calling out to me I don't dare look at him either. The disappointment in their eyes would kill me as surely as a silver bullet.

I avoid Mica's worried stare as she passes me a few scraps of food on my way though the kitchen. I fold the napkin around her offerings and hold them tight as Mario takes me to my cell. He's speaking quietly to me, but with the pounding in my head, I can't quite make out what he's saying. He leads me down the stairs and goes instantly silent when he sees Sandy in her cell. That's when his words register in my brain.

I still have the key!

Thinking about it now renews my purpose and fills me with a measure of hope. I can use it tonight to get to the master's main office. Once I get hold of the master key, I'll be able to free everyone and flee this place before I'm forced to lead a team of handlers to Logan's family.

My wolf howls and my heart races as I settle on my cot. The master might have won the battle of wills today in the courtyard, but if he thinks he's beaten me, or worse broken me, he has another thought coming.

There's still hope.

With Sandy watching me, I try to keep my blood steady and work to wipe the excitement from my face, but when Mario meets my glance, and I see a glimmer of understanding in his eyes, we exchange a knowing look.

We're getting out of here tonight.

Once Mario is gone, I tuck into my food, and even though my stomach is clenching, I know I'll need the energy for tonight and all the roadblocks I'll have to find a way to cross. Knowing Sandy has eaten well today after winning her race, I nibble slowly on the cheese, and place the meat on the warm slice of bread before I eat it.

I turn to look at the young wolf. She's lying on her side, her head propped on her hand, and she's giving me an odd look, like she senses a change about me.

"Sandy," I begin trying to keep my voice steady as I prepare her for tonight's events, being careful not to give away too much information, or frighten her off. "Have you ever thought about getting out of here? Of running in the mountain?"

Something flickers in her eyes, and for a moment I recognize the old Sandy, the young pup with so much hope and life. "It's too dangerous out there. There are too many threats," she answers and rolls onto her back and her wild curls fall around her shoulders. "The master keeps us safe inside here. You should be grateful."

"What if I can take you to a place where it is safe? Where you can run free and not worry about any threats."

Her gaze jerks back to mine. "Where's that?"

I go quiet for a moment, worried about how much to reveal. "Just say I can. Would you go?"

She rolls until her back is facing me, but I see the fear in her eyes before she turns away, and it's that fear that tells me she's been through so much in the last month.

Her tone is clipped when she says, "We shouldn't be having this conversation."

My heart drops into my stomach and the worry I hear in her voice makes me ever determined to help her.

Time passes slowly as I wait for Sandy to fall asleep, and when I finally hear her breathing level out and regulate, I know it's time to make my move.

My pulse jumps as I push off my ratty blanket and drop to the floor. I give Sandy one quick last look before I lift the corner of my cot to retrieve the hidden key. Except when I pull the mattress back, I can't quite seem to locate it.

Panic sets my heart racing, and I push the cot back even farther, thinking perhaps it had shifted beneath the mattress, or fallen to the floor. I search frantically in the dark, but when my hands come out empty, a cry lodges in my throat.

It's gone!

I jump up, and search around my dusty cement floor, not wanting to believe I've lost it, or worse, someone found it.

But who?

"It's for your own good," Sandy says, without turning to face me.

I run to the cage and grip the bars. "Sandy, no. You have to give it to me." I rattle the bars hard, demanding she turn to look at me so I can convince her that I know what's best.

"Go to sleep, Pride."

Dark despair churns inside me and I yell at her, desperate to get through to her. My heart hammers as I shake the cage harder, but the more I protest the more she works at ignoring me. When she pulls her blanket over her head, I switch tactics and tell her about my time in the mountains, the running, the freedom, and how her babies won't suffer the way she's suffered, but no matter how hard I plead I still can't seem to get through to her.

I hear a loud noise upstairs and as fear rushes up my spine I scurry back to my bunk, wondering what all the commotion is about. Then I hear what can only be gunshots and I press my back to the cold wall and pull my legs to my chest. A loud wail rises from my throat and I wonder, who is the master torturing now? When the mansion shakes again I worry for Logan, Stone, all the other wolves and even the staff who have no more control over their lives than I do.

Despite the adrenaline pumping through my veins I suddenly feel very weary, very lost. As emotions get the better of me, I can feel tears fill my eyes. The room blurs before me and I wonder if I'm simply fighting a losing battle. I look at Sandy, then think of all the new wolves in the courtyard, the ones who pushed me around because I somehow threatened their master—my father. Perhaps Stone was right all along. Perhaps these broken wolves can't be saved because they don't want to be saved.

Maybe I never should have returned. Maybe I should have heeded Stone's warning and stayed away. Then Logan's family never would have been put danger, or worse, gone missing. Gem never would have been captured and my mate never would have been tortured.

Now it was all for nothing, because the key to my escape is just out of reach and come tomorrow morning I'll have no choice but to lead the master to the small colony in the Canadian mountains. Guilt overwhelms me and an invisible fist squeezes my heart, because I might as well be pulling the trigger and pumping Logan's family full of silver myself.

What have I done?

My tears fall heavier now, soaking my face and blanket and I don't bother wiping them away. I sniff loudly but there is nothing I can do to get myself under control. Soon my soft cries turn into big hiccupping sobs and I realize I'm falling apart, completely collapsing under the weight of failure.

Is this what it feels like to be broken?

I can feel myself sinking deeper and deeper, drowning in pool of despair and this time I let it pull me under like a deadly wave, let it fill my lungs until they're starved for oxygen. As emotions erupt inside me I suddenly hate Logan.

Hate that he believed in me.

Hate that he put this kind of responsibility on me.

Hate that I'm letting him down.

I pound on my bed and cry harder.

"Pride."

I go silent and listen, wondering if I'm hearing things or if someone is in the cellar calling my name. I swallow and wipe my nose as I peer into the dark and look for movement.

"Pride," the voice comes again, and I see Sandy sitting up in her cot, her head darting from left to right, trying to figure out what is going.

I climb from my bed and pad to my door. "Who's there?" I ask quietly.

When a tall figure comes out of the shadows I suck in air and falter backwards.

When I hit the back of my cage, my body goes instantly stiff, and my heart thunders. "Go away," I say as fresh tears sting my eyes.

He shakes his head and comes closer to my cage. "You need to hear me out."

"I've heard all I need to know," I shoot back and press against the bars, unable to put any more distance between us.

"Please let me explain, Pride."

"Explain? You want to explain why you left your wife and child in a place like this while you ran a prison of your own. Do you somehow think there is something you can say to make that okay in my eyes?"

"It was never supposed to be like this," he begins and his voice is low, soft, full of pain. "For many years I was a rogue wolf, one who had no morals and didn't know right from wrong. When I met your master we were both young and hungry for money and blood."

I think back to what Stone told me. That my father was a powerful alpha and maybe he was the one controlling the master. I wave my hand. "So this was all your idea then?"

He nods and his honesty is like a knife to the jugular. I step farther away from him, confused and fearful but mostly angry.

"We built an army and we became rich and powerful." He lowers his head like he's reliving a distant time. "Then I met your mother, and I fell in love."

At the mention of my mother a howl sounds in my throat. I point to the floorboards above my head. "He killed her and you didn't do anything about it."

His gaze jerks back to mine and his eyes are pleading. "I didn't know, Pride. It wasn't until long after he killed her that I found out."

"Well you know now, which makes me wonder how you can even sit and have a conversation with him, acting like you're old friends after what he did to my mother—a woman you supposedly loved."

"Not supposedly. I did love her. And I love you."

I think about Logan, Stone, the elders and all the sacrifices they made for me. "Don't talk to me about love. You know nothing about it."

"That's where you're wrong, my little girl."

"Don't call me that. I'm not your little girl. I'm not your anything."

"Pride—"

"If you loved us so much then why did you leave?"

"Your master started changing. He became greedy, cruel. Dangerous."

Fire erupts in my belly and I give a hard shake of my head, my blonde curls flying around my face. "So you thought it would be a good idea to just leave us with a man like that then?"

"Do you remember I once said some things are worse than death?" There is something deeply desperate in his voice that gains my attention.

I don't answer. I just stand there and stare at him until he continues. "I left to protect you. Your master was becoming strong, more powerful that I ever would have imagined, and he was learning about us, learning how to manipulate the wolves inside us. When he realized he could use our empathy against us, I knew he could never know how I really felt about you or your mother. You were safer with me gone."

I pinch the bridge of my nose and can feel the fight drain out of me. "Why are you here? What do you want from me?"

"I want to help."

"It's a little late for that don't you think?" I shoot back.

"You're smart, Pride. You know we're building an army, but do you know why?"

"I know there are panthers stalking the compound."

He nods. "There's a turf war going on. A cartel is moving in from the south and they want to take over. They know we harbor wolves, and somehow they managed to find and harness panthers to do their bidding. Your master thought he had more time."

"Which is why he's breeding the females and hoping to harness Logan's family."

"Right. But he's out of time. We all are."

My pulse leaps. "What are you talking about?"

"We're under attack."

I hear Sandy make a gasping sound and my numb feet slide across the cold floor. I step up to my father to meet his gaze, to read his body language. But there is nothing to suggest he's lying.

"What's going on?" I ask.

"The panthers are closing in."

I think back to the gun shots I heard earlier. "They have guns?"

"No. The PTF tracked them here. To complicate things, your master has some of the PTF officers in his pocket so we don't know who's on our side and who isn't."

As far as I'm concerned the PTF are never on our side. I grip the bars tighter as panic erupts inside me.

"There is one more thing you need to know."

I swallow, not liking the sound of that. "Your master has left you all here to your own fate. He's in his office making arrangements to get to his helicopter on the rooftop." He goes quiet for a moment then he says, "And he has Gem with him."

"Gem! Why?" I blurt out. "Why would he want Gem?"

"Because he's broken her, and now she can lead him to her family in the Canadian mountains."

My brain races to catch up because I know I'm missing something here. "Isn't it a little too late for that?"

"No. If he can harness them, he can start over again some-where else."

I look around frantically. "I need to get out of here." I

turn to Sandy. Her mouth is agape and her eyes are wide. "Sandy—" I begin but my father cuts me off.

"You'll need this."

A cry of relief lodges in my throat when he produces the master key. "We need to free everyone, but how are we going to get out of here with the panthers closing in?"

"The tunnels. I can lead them to safety."

Then it dawns on me. That's how he's been getting into my quarters, through the underground tunnels. And he knows about the secret passageways because he's the one who helped the master design them.

But I can't think about that right now. Right now I have to find the master and stop him before he gets away with Gem.

Once my father unlocks our cages, he gestures with a nod. "We can get to all the others this way, and then we can get to safety at the top of the mountain."

My feet come to a skidding halt as a new plan begins to unravel in my brain. "You free your pack of wolves, then give the key to Mario. The handler is on our side and Stone trusts him. The master's wolves will go with Stone before they'll go with you."

I see worry in his eyes. "What are you saying?"

As hot emotions rush through my blood I draw a breath to steady myself and remember my purpose. A new calmness falls over me and I step away from my father.

I think of my mother, Jace and Clover. They all fought for me, stayed brave for me and I'm not about to cower in the face of death and let the sacrifices they made go unavenged. As I let the decision settle into my brain I think about the vow I made a long time ago. I came back to get these wolves out of this prison alive, and I plan to do that even if it means trading my life for theirs.

Because I understand what my father had been trying to

tell me and why he left the compound. Putting those you love in harm's way, simply because you love them is far worse than death.

Stone understood this very thing. Which is why he always pretended to be my enemy.

"What I'm saying is I'm not going with you," I inform him and shudder as the weight of the decision settles around me.

"Pride," he warns.

"You free the others and get to safety. I have some unfinished business to take care of."

15

Giving my father no time to protest, I climb to the top of my cage and disappear into the ventilation system. As I move through the ducts I feel the house shake from some sort of explosion and as I hold the metal walls to brace myself I realized just how desperate the situation has become.

Once the house stops vibrating I bolt forward on my hands and knees, twisting and turning until I come upon the master's suite. I take a quick look inside and when I see him with Gem, I kick the shaft clear from the wall and drop down in front of them. I take on a combative stance, and my lips peel back to expose sharp canines.

The master turns on me, and surprise lights his eyes. My consideration goes to Gem, who looks battered and beaten, the gleam gone from her once vibrant eyes. The sight of her rouses my wolf and my nails elongate.

The master's dark bark of laughter has my head swinging back to him. "Well, well," he says as his focus goes from me to the broken vent back to me again. "Let me guess, your daddy had something to do with this." He scoffs and continues, "I should have known. And really, I never should have expected a traitor like him to give birth to anything but a runt, anyway."

I can tell he's trying to taunt me, to throw me off my game so he can escape before I shift. But what he doesn't realize is I'm no longer the little girl who thought of her size as a weakness. Thanks to Logan, I've come a long way since escaping here.

He grabs Gem's arm harder, hauling her against his chest. She makes a frightened, squeaking sound and it prompts me into action but I slow a little when he uses her small body to shield his. I take one threatening step toward him yet he continues to hold his ground, the laughter fading from his eyes, which are now hard, raw with anger.

"You never were a threat to me, Pride."

"You're not going to get away with what you've done to us."

I take a moment to assess Gem, to figure out how to stage an attack on the master without her getting caught in the crossfire, but when I see her green eyes glittering beneath the black bleakness and she mouths the word grasshopper, understanding hits me over the head like a mallet.

Grasshopper is her safe word!

My heart leaps with joy. Gem isn't broken and this is her way of letting me know she's okay. She's stronger than I ever knew and that she had the foresight to plant a safe word at the beginning of this journey shows just how brilliant she really is.

I give a slight nod to signal my understanding, and don't miss the small grin that pulls at her lips. I also realize from the gray pallor of her skin that she's still feverish, which is preventing her from shifting and fighting back. But at least I know she's going to be okay. Now I just have to figure out how to free her.

I turn my attention back to the master and he gives a shake of his head. "You know, your downfall has always been the way you care for other. You might have made a powerful leader one day, Pride." He stops to let his disapproving glance rake over me. "But then again, how much I can really expect from a runt like you?"

Before I get the chance to show him, an explosion rocks the mansion and rips a hole in the floor beneath me. Dust flies into the air, and I choke on the particles. I wave my arms to clear the debris, but when I do I notice the master is gone, Gem with him. It's then that I notice the hidden door at the back of his office. Before it locks behind him, I bolt forward and thanks to my small size I'm able to slip inside before it closes.

I hear footsteps on the stairs, and my ears perk as I follow the sound. I take the steps two at a time, my wolf clamoring to break free but I know I can't let her out just yet. We might have more obstacles to conquer before I can let her off her leash.

From somewhere up above I hear a door bang open and slam shut, and assume they've reached the rooftop. When I finally reach the top, I approach the door with caution, not knowing who or what is waiting for me on the other side.

Using my shoulder I nudge it open and take a second to assess the situation. But when I hear footsteps thundering on the stairs below me, I know I have to make a move because it sounds like the PTF is closing in.

I dart onto the roof in time to see the master and Gem climb into the helicopter, the master at the controls. Using every ounce of strength I possess, I run for the airliner but when the door behind me opens and I hear, "Stop," I spin around in time to see a gun pointed at my head.

My heart thunders because I instantly recognize the man with the gun trained on me. It's the PTF officer I took down in Olympic National Park. The same one my wolf nearly tore to shreds but stopped at the last second.

I growl at him as the helicopter's blades begin to spin. I need to move and I need to do it now, but the minute I turn my back on him, will he shoot it full of silver? I gauge the time it will take me to reach the helicopter and can only hope I can free Gem and kill the master before the silver poising takes effect, because I've come too far to let anyone stand in my way.

I'm about to move, but something in the man's face changes, softens and when he speaks I can barely believe what he's saying.

"You spared my life. Now I'm sparing yours."

As my brain deciphers his words I realize he's working with me, not against me. Without any time to give it further consideration I spin around and jump on the skids moments before the helicopter makes lift. With strength I never knew I had, I pull the door clear off its hinges.

The master's eyes go wide. "What is this—" he begins.

But I grab him by the collar and say, "This, my dear master, is what you can expect from a runt like me." Then I haul him from the helicopter and send him tumbling to the ground. When Gem jumps free, I pounce on the master, and my wolf howls in sheer delight, because she knows.

She knows I'm finally going to let her off her leash.

I pin the master to the ground beneath me, and my mouth salivates, ready to call on my wolf so she can rip into his throat and watch the life drain out of him. But when I listen to the animal cries in the distance, it does something to me. I lift my head and as I scent the air my attention goes to the PTF officer who is watching me carefully. The sight of him reminds me that I'm better than this. I might be a wolf, raised as an assassin by a cruel man, but I'm not monster.

Inside I'm just a seventeen-year-old girl who wants to live a normal life.

My wolf wails as I push off the master and climb to shaky feet. He scrambles backwards and rises. As I draw a calming breath, desperate to settle my wolf, I move between him and the helicopter, blocking his path. With panthers closing in from the stairwell I know he has nowhere to go. I turn to see Gem watching me.

"Pride?" she questions.

"The panthers are coming," I say, breathless, as I wipe my mouth with the back of my hand. "Let's leave his fate in his own hands."

With that I turn to look at the PTF officer, determined to make something clear. "We're not the monsters," I say.

He nods and moves toward me. "I know."

"There are other compounds."

"We're searching now."

"So you're going to—"

"Yes," he says. "Our unit has assembled a new task force."

Just then the roof door swings open and out struts two sleek black panthers. They sniff the air like feral bloodhounds on a hunt, and when they catch the master's scent, they stalk toward him, completely ignoring us three. The master falters and falls backwards. When he lands with a thump he begins pleading for his life, but the panthers never falter. They begin circling, closing the berth.

The officer grabs my arm. "We need to move."

I reach for Gem and catch her hand as the officer races toward the helicopter.

We jump in and I look at the controls frantically. "Do you know how to fly this?"

He nods. "Years of training. All a part of the special task force."

Over the loud hum of the blades I can hear the master

howling, but when I think about all the abuse so many have suffered at his hands, I refuse to feel sympathy for him.

When we take to the air, I don't look back, instead I focus on the ground, and on the future before me. "What about all the panthers that have been unleashed?" I ask. "They're not like us."

"We have a mess on our hands, but now that we know what we're up against, we can figure out a way to deal with it." He carries us up the mountain and when he finally lands at the top of the vineyard, he powers down the machine and gestures toward the rolling hills with a nod. "You need to get out of here."

I peer into the night, swallow hard and say, "Thank you."

I jump from my seat, and Gem steps up beside me. Before we lose ourselves in the dark, the officer says, "Take care of yourselves."

As emotions choke me I grab Gem's hand and we walk away in search of our family. When we finally spot them near the cannon, I see my father, his wolves, Sandy and all the staff. I'm not surprised to find Lawrence standing there and note he doesn't look so tough anymore. I look through the throngs of wolves behind them and search for Logan and Stone, but when I don't see them my heart goes into my throat.

A few minutes later, when we finally step up to them, my expression is stricken. I turn questioning eyes on my father, and he says, "They both went looking for you."

I spin around. "They're in danger, I have to go back."

I make a step to go, but my father grabs my arm. "Wait."

I turn back to see him and he's smiling, then I follow his gaze. I cry out in relief when I see Logan and Stone cresting the hill.

My head goes back and forth between the two boys who mean so much to me, but when my glance settles on Logan and I see the raw hate in his eyes, my heart seizes. But it's not me he's looking at, it's my father.

Before I know what's happening, I see a flurry of activity and Logan starts running. Brutally fast, he pounces and slams my father to the ground. His canines punch through his gums and when his loud growls serrate the quiet and reverberate off the mountain, fear for my father's life has me screaming.

"Logan, don't," I yell, and realize that Logan has no idea who this man is. "He's my father," I explain.

Logan bares his teeth and looks at me. "Pride?" he questions with a growl. "He was *my* master."

That revelation takes me by surprise. I know Logan spent time in a compound but I had no idea he was ruled by my father. Then I remember something very important Logan once said to me when he saw my deep scars. He said his master wasn't so cruel. That gives me a measure of comfort to know my father ruled with a softer hand.

"Logan," I begin gently as he climbs to his feet. "If it wasn't for him, we never would have gotten out alive."

Pewter bleeds into his gorgeous blue eyes as his wolf continues to hunger for my father's blood. "You're just going to forgive him for all he's done?"

"I don't know anything about forgiveness," I say quietly and step up to him so I can put my palm on his face, letting him know how much I care about him. "But sometimes we have to do what we have to do. I understand that now."

His hand closes over mine. "Pride, are you sure?"

I step back and my gaze goes from Logan to Stone and his eyes are asking the question that his lips can't.

Who will I pick?

I don't directly answer but I think the two alphas who I've grown to love know what I mean when I say. "Actually, I'm not sure about anything anymore." In a crucial first step of discovery, I move closer to my father, understanding that I still have so much to learn about my past, my future, my family, my world, but most importantly, myself.

Before I make any decisions that will affect the rest of my life, I have to stand by the only man who can best help me find my way.

And I know the two boys who I care about the most, two wolves who would fight to the death to save me, might not like my choices, but I know them both well enough to know they'll respect them.

EPILOGUE

fter crossing the border with the necessary identification in hand, all thanks to Mario and his illegal connections, we make our way to Logan's small, secluded town in the Canadian mountains—a place where we can only hope that Malcolm and the others are alive and safe.

I can't deny that I'm excited to live a normal life and happiness swells inside me as I look at my new family: my father, Logan, Stone, Gem and Sandy, as well as a few other wolves who've decided to come with us.

The rest of the pack stayed behind, most searching for their long lost families while the others simply wanted to start fresh.

Mario and the staff stayed behind as well and it makes me happy to know they can now live the lives they've always wanted. My father, who is desperate to right his wrongs, provided everyone with enough money to get them on their feet.

I turn my focus to the future ahead of me, but as we approach Logan's community the scent of smoke hits me hard. I turn to see a worried look in Logan's eyes. I slip my hand into his and he looks at me, his blue eyes troubled.

"Maybe it's nothing," I say as an uneasy feeling closes in on me.

"Maybe," he responds as our feet slap the pavement, but the closer we get, the stronger the scent grows. Smoke begins to saturate the air and when we finally crest the hill overlooking his small town, I suck in a huge breath and a cry lodges in my throat.

"Logan," I say my stomach clenching.

He throws his head back. "No," he wails and his loud distress howl cuts the quiet of the night.

Tears sting my eyes and I wrap my arms around him and hold him tight as guilt eats at me. This is my fault. I never should have let his family fight my battle.

"I'm so sorry," I say.

With our world collapsing, I look at the charred houses and the burned community in chaos. Anger boils my blood and I know in an instant our fight for freedom, our fight to prove *we're* not the monsters is far from over.

AFTERWORD

Thank You!

Thank you so much for reading Pride Unleashed, book two in my Pride series. I hope you enjoyed the story as much as I loved writing it. Please read on for an excerpt of Pride;s Pursuit, available now.

Interested in leaving a review? Please do! Reviews help readers connect with books that work for them. I appreciate all reviews, whether positive or negative.

Happy Reading,
    Cathryn

PRIDE'S PURSUIT

After defeating her master and releasing the enslaved wolves, Pride, Logan, Stone and the rest of the pack return to the Canadian mountains only to discover a village in chaos. Feeling responsible for the carnage, Pride is determined to show the world exactly who the monsters really are.

When her pack refuses to let her fight alone, Pride and her team set out to change mankind. But when her leadership is tested and a traitor emerges, not only must Pride pick between the two boys who love her most, her choice could either help put an end to war on the wolves or it could endanger the very existence of her kind.

Chapter One

The fire has been burning for days, the savage blaze devouring everything in its drunken path. Wild, angry flames lick the star-studded sky as plumes of smoke form an eerie haze over the waxing moon, turning the night an ominous shade of red.

Chalky ash falls from the treetops like the winter's first

snow and the scent of blood is so thick in the air it twists my stomach and clogs my dry throat. I wince as the bitter taste of death settles on the back of my tongue and burns my flesh like hot, molten silver.

At the crest of this secluded mountain town there are no fire trucks to be seen, no blaring alarms to be heard. Without a team of brave firefighters here to extinguish the inferno, I fear it could go on forever.

Hot panic is the first thing I feel. Anger is the second. It churns inside my gut, and the feral wolf inside me turns vicious as she takes in the senseless chaos unfolding before her eyes.

I breathe deep to move past the coppery tang of blood and smoke and that's when I catch a familiar scent, one that reminds me of rotten eggs and car exhaust. My pulse drums harder in my neck while my brain weeds through the smells, shifting and sorting until it's able to determine the true root of the odor.

Gasoline.

I give a hard shake of my head, my rattled brain struggling to come up with some plausible explanation as to who or what could have doused the village with fuel.

How was this secret town discovered?

I mull that over for a moment longer, and then suddenly my thoughts come to a screeching halt; the only reasonable answer lodging in my esophagus like a lump of day old bread.

"No," I cry out, my breath coming quicker now, the world around me blurring in and out of existence while waves of blistering heat wash over my trembling body. As the fire sucks the oxygen from the air, bile punches into my throat and it takes two locked knees to keep my legs from failing.

My hackles spike and a deep howl rents the air. The low-pitch sound chases the flames up the mountain only to get lost in the thick underbrush. Acrid smoke stings my eyes and I blink against its toxic bite as I quickly assess the damage. My head jerks from left to right and the brisk autumn breeze fueling the flames whips my curls across my face.

I push my hair from my watery eyes and strive to gather my thoughts. But before I can settle the chaos bouncing around inside my brain like a puppy's rubber chew toy, the shifters at my back bolt forward, leaving Logan and me alone in the bleak night.

A split second later—my father, Stone, Gem and Sandy—the wolves who travelled to Canada with Logan and me disappear from my line of sight, four brave warriors charging head first into the inferno. Even though I can't seem to move my legs, can't seem to follow them into the flames, the commotion pulls a reaction from my wolf.

Thick talons elongate, and her unchecked rage jumps a few notches, her animal instincts feeding off the dark destruction closing in on her. Deep inside she wails, clamoring to be unleashed. Her loud primal cry is a clear indication that she knows. She knows the person responsible for the destruction of Logan's entire village. His entire family.

That person is me.

While I might not have been the one to soak the village in gasoline, might not have been the one to ignite the match that lit the town on fire, I know this damage is my fault. I'm smart enough to understand this violence is a direct result of my escape from the compound a month ago, when the Paranormal Task Force chased me through Olympic National Park.

I have no doubt in my mind that the PTF officers—men who shoot first and ask questions later—tracked me to this private village, a place where werewolves live normal lives and take to the woods on shift night to avoid bloodshed.

It's the only logical explanation.

My hands fist at my sides and my heart pounds as rage unfurls inside me. This wasn't supposed to happen! None of this was supposed to happen. After freeing the pack of wolves trapped in our cruel master's cellar, six of us fled the California compound together and travelled to Logan's secluded home in the Canadian mountains with one purpose in mind.

To live normal lives.

But as I stare at the devastation, the complete and utter destruction of his entire community, I realize that as long as the PTF are out there, as long as they believe we are cold-blooded killers who feast on flesh and must be destroyed, we'll never be free.

I want to scream. I want to cry. I want to kill the officers who refuse to believe we can live normal lives. Refuse to believe we're not beasts, out to turn innocent humans into blood lusting monsters who kill for sport. What is it going to take for them to understand that we're not soulless predators?

I take a moment to process and when the full impact of what really happened here hits like a sucker punch, my stomach cramps and I nearly vomit. I swallow hard and my ears perk as dry tinder pops and splinters beneath the fiery assault, the sound reverberating off the distant, snow-packed peaks.

But soon the noise is drowned out by the deep, tortured howl coming from the boy beside me—a selfless boy who crawled straight into my hell to save me from certain death. I never should have drawn him into my dark world. If I hadn't accepted his help, the help of his family, then none of this would be happening.

When I see the horror in his blue eyes, and taste the bite of his fury as it pollutes the heavy air and mingles with black wisps of smoke, my anger turns to worry.

"Logan," I rush out, forcing my heavy legs to move so I can go to him. "Logan, I'm so sorry."

"You don't have anything to be sorry for." There is a definite edge to his voice, one fed by pure desperation, when he whispers through clenched teeth, "But whoever did this does."

Looking hard and dangerously feral, he angles his head unnaturally. Flecks of pewter puncture the blue in his eyes as they lock on mine, but judging from his wild, distant stare, I get the sense that it's not really me he's seeing.

The tormented look moving over his face is beyond frightening and as I take in the tension in his normally relaxed posture, equal amounts of fear and worry slither through my bloodstream like a poisonous snake. The truth is I've seen this boy beaten to within an inch of his life, yet never have I been so afraid for him.

Understanding his world is collapsing around him, I pinch back the tears stinging my eyes and touch his arm in an effort to bring his attention back to me.

"Logan," I say softly, knowing he may very well have lost everyone he's ever cared about and right now needs me to be the voice of calm, not anger. I temporarily shelve the rage inside me—a rage that is prompting me to find the men who did this and tear their heads clear from their bodies—so I can focus solely on what Logan needs from me.

"Pride," he whispers and pulls me to him. His hold is fierce, his embrace so tight it forces out what little oxygen I have left in my lungs. His voice echoes desperately inside my head as he buries his face in my disheveled hair. His breathing is rough, labored and I can feel his heart pound against my chest.

"Pride," he murmurs again, his voice shaking worse than his hands. I hold him tighter and can feel his enraged wolf prowling restlessly inside him, urging him to shift.

To kill.

"I'm here," I assure him, pain stabbing my heart like a double edged blade. I try to reach out to him mentally, to help soothe the dark distress eating him up inside. Despite our connection, an intimate bond that developed from trust while we struggled to survive together in the forest, I still can't speak to him telepathically.

"Everything is going to be okay," I say for lack of anything else, even though I know nothing is ever going to be okay again, especially if his entire family has been burned and left for dead.

When his hands fist my hair, my fingers curl in his t-shirt. The chaos around us fades to a distant buzz and as we cling to one another his warm familiar scent almost makes me feel safe. Almost.

As I offer whatever comfort I can, I listen to his blood rush and despite the urgency of the situation we stay like that for a long moment, until a hard voice forces us to separate. I step back, but my wolf bristles, not wanting to break from Logan.

"*Pride*," Stone says, his deep guttural voice sweeping through my thoughts like the brush fire through the pines. I edge farther away from Logan, severing the connection as I turn to Stone.

He looks at me for a long moment, his eyes clouding with savage emotion before he says, "Y*our father wants you.*" Firelight illuminates his strong features as he speaks telepathically to me, a means of communication, I recently learned, that only true mates are capable of establishing while in their human form.

But now is not the time to be worrying about all the secrets that have been kept from me since birth, not when Logan's world is falling apart around him.

Stone inches closer, each step calculated, purposeful.

Predatory.

Fear shoots through me and the hairs on my nape prickle when I see worry tightening his features. His anxiety wraps around me like a lethal serpent and squeezes so hard I can feel my heart constrict to the point of pain.

I suck in a sharp breath and try not to cough as my lungs fill with smoke. "What is it?" I ask, forcing the words past my lips so I don't exclude Logan from our conversation.

He takes another measured step closer and I can feel the warmth of his body as his knuckles slide along mine. There is something very primal and raw in his eyes as they study me darkly. A moment passes before he finally answers me.

"We found someone. She's alive." His glance shifts to Logan and for the first time I don't see black hatred in his dark expression. And it's that lack of hatred that has me worried.

Stone, the alpha wolf who was destined to be my true mate, straightens to his full height and expands his chest as he makes eye contact with Logan, the boy I gave myself to—body and heart—during the last full moon.

Stone's forehead creases, the seriousness of the situation apparent in his expression. "You'd better come with us. She's asking for you."

Logan's eyes widen, a deadly tornado brewing in their stormy depths. "Who is it?" he rushes out.

"I don't know. She's not talking."

Logan makes a step to go, but Stone moves in front of him to block his path. His actions appear threatening to Logan's wolf, and I draw in a sharp breath when Logan assumes a combative stance.

With his body on edge, his every muscle tight, Stone searches the other boy's face. A hush falls over us, even the animals scurrying from the fire go mute as the two alphas glare at one another, their gazes clashing in a silent battle of wills. With my pulse jack hammering, I tense at the strained silence, and watch, transfixed, wondering what Stone is trying to prove.

This is not the time to be fighting for pack control!

But when he pitches his voice low and says, "She's hurt pretty badly," preparing his enemy for the horror he's about to face, my heart squeezes in my chest. Stone might be a hard alpha, a trained killer who's been caged and tortured his whole life, but deep inside he's just a boy.

One who is as lost as I am.

Logan gives a curt nod and when Stone steps back Logan takes the opportunity to bolt forward. I immediately chase after him and stay close, keeping pace as the grief-stricken alpha makes his way to his village. But soon his long legs are covering a vast amount of ground and I'm unable to keep up. Stone lags behind and runs by my side, his shrewd eyes trained on my back. Watching me.

Always watching me.

Wind whips at my face as I steal a sideways glance at him. Speaking telepathically, I begin, *"Are they all...?"* But then I stop abruptly, unable to push any more words out. I don't need to finish the sentence for Stone to know what I'm asking, anyway. Even without making a mental connection, he can read my thoughts and actions as well as I can read his.

"I don't know. We only found the girl and she's not speaking."

I push harder, my feet slapping a steady beat against the hot road beneath me. Since we ditched our car long ago, not wanting to take a chance that my father's vehicle could be tracked to Logan's home, the final trek up the twisting mountain has to be made on foot.

The noise of my shoes pounding pavement echoes in the night and drowns out the hum of my heavy panting. Moisture breaks out on my skin, and my heart begins to beat so fast I fear it's going to burst from my chest. But I don't let that stop me. I can't. Worry for Logan and what he might find prompts me to dig my heels in deeper. There is no way I'm going to let him face this senseless brutality alone.

Just because I recently distanced myself from the alphas —deciding for all our sakes that I need to find myself and learn about my past before I can commit to my future—it doesn't mean that I don't care for the two boys. I do.

A lot.

We breeze by an abandoned playground. The rusty hinges on the old swing set squeal like a wounded animal as it sways in the night breeze. My heart clenches when I think of the children, a community lost, destroyed by cruel men who fear what they don't know. What they don't understand.

From everything I've witnessed over the last few weeks, it's become glaringly apparent to me that the PTF are nothing but trained assassins, more merciless than the wolves they hunt.

Then again, I can't forget about the one officer who saved my life after I spared his. But I very much doubt he can change the minds of many, not without some sort of proof that we're not simply out for blood. But how can we prove that, and how many more will die until we find a way?

My steps slow and Logan's hushed voice cuts through the chaos and reaches my ears as we approach a burned out building. Before I push my way into one of the fire-ravaged structures, Stone catches my hand in a firm hold.

My gaze darts to his and when his brow creases in concern, I note the ways his muscles are bunching, rippling along his shoulders and down his arms. His jaw seesaws from side to side, and I instantly brace myself, because I know that look.

I know what it means.

He inches closer, his body crowding mine. "I don't think you should go in," he warns.

I give a fierce shake of my head and my teeth clamp hard enough to chip bone. "Well I think I should," I counter and snatch my hand back from his tight grip.

While I understand it's in Stone's nature to protect me, and I wouldn't be alive today without his intelligence or sheer strength of character, he needs to understand that in the outside world, he can no longer be my strength.

I love and admire him for his protectiveness and intellect, I really do. And while I know he's a creature of habit, ruled by his survival instincts, I also know if we are going to thrive in a place where compound rules no longer apply, he has to allow me to grow, to find my path, and to respect my choices instead of trying to make them for me.

Looking rattled, he rakes his hands through his mussed hair and everything inside me reaches out to him, my heart aching for the tormented alpha and all he's been through.

"*Pride*—" he begins, his voice a low, strained whisper as he makes a mental connection, and I instantly harden myself.

Knowing it's for Stone's own good—the good of our kind —I tilt my chin and glare at him with stubborn determination.

"This isn't up for debate," I say, my voice low, but unwavering.

He glares at me, then understanding I'm not about to back down, he disengages himself from my thoughts and gives a resigned shake of his head. Still I know he'll follow me.

With that I turn and push a broken and charred door out of my way. It falls to the floor and the noise shudders in the unnatural silence. Instincts on high alert, I step inside and my taste buds are instantly assaulted with the decaying stench of charred flesh. My gut clenches and my wolf howls in response, the smell so overwhelming that I have to breathe through my mouth to avoid choking.

Pushing on, I carefully pick my way through burnt debris, my feet falling mutely as I step over black beams and scorched floorboards. The house is dark, all but destroyed, the rooms lit only by the few orange embers still smoldering in the structure's outer edges.

With my senses guiding the way, I go deeper into the house, or at least what's still standing of it. The floor creaks and I fear it's about to collapse beneath Stone's impressive weight. He keeps close to me, so close I can feel his warm breath on my neck. We continue forward until I find the others in a room that once served as a kitchen.

Dread takes hold when I see a badly beaten girl—one who is no older than me. Crouched on the floor with her back braced against a seared wall, her breath is coming in quick, labored bursts.

Everything from the vacant look in her pale blue eyes, to the way her legs are pulled to her chest, her arms hugging them tightly against her bloody body, warns that she's still paralyzed with fear. The sour stench of her terror, a pungent mixture of curdled milk and spoiled meat, has the animal in me howling with rage, eager to seek revenge on those who did this to her.

As I pull in the scent, allowing it to fuel my wolf, Logan kneels in front of her. Talking in soft, whispered words he carefully brushes her ragged hair from her face. My perked ears enable me to listen in on the hushed conversation.

Not wanting to startle the girl I move in beside my father. I tilt my head to meet his glance and when I do his dark eyes narrow in genuine concern. After we exchange a worried look, I take in the stricken expressions of the other shifters in our pack. When my glance meets Gem's I gesture with a nod to Sandy, who looks paler than ever as she rubs the small bulge in her expanding belly.

Knowing this is no place for a girl in her condition and

that her growing child shouldn't be exposed to any of the toxic fumes still lingering in the air, I jerk my head toward the doorway.

Gem instantly understands my message and leads Sandy outside. Once she's gone, I turn my attention back to Logan. Driven by pure instinct, I take a small step closer to him, my wolf needing in the most desperate ways to support the alpha she mated with. But when I do, the girl flinches. Undisguised panic ripples through her, and she pulls Logan against her, shielding her body with his.

"It's okay, Nova," he murmurs as he slides me a look that speaks volumes. While we might not be able to speak mentally, I know him well enough to understand what he's asking of me. I give a tight nod and inch back until I'm once again standing next to my father. After giving Logan and the girl a generous amount of space, Nova relaxes slightly, but she still doesn't ease her hold on the alpha.

"It's Pride," he explains, his voice both soft and soothing as he settles his own emotions so he can concentrate on Nova. My heart lurches, remembering all the techniques this boy once used to relieve my worries and gain my trust. While he might be young, his intuition and inner strength never fail to amaze me. "You remember Pride, don't you?" he asks.

Nova's jerky nod takes me by surprise. Her thick, death-black hair falls forward and masks her features as I study her harder, struggling to figure out who she is, and how she knows me. Before the answer comes to me, Logan slowly climbs to his feet, and his voice gives way to soft persuasion as he coaxes her to follow him up.

Her bones crack in protest as she stands and I wonder how long she's been crouched in that same position. Looking badly beaten and frightened to the point of tears her eyes rake over the motley crew with detached interest. But when her glance lands on me and lingers for longer than what's comfortable, I get the strangest sense that she's sizing me up.

Unease moves into my stomach and my hackles bristle. The dark warning shivering through my blood has my wolf growling. But I place my hand over my stomach to hush her.

Logan curls a protective arm around the girl's shoulders and pulls her against him to offer comfort. She melts into him and that's when her identity hits me. I'd briefly met her at Logan's house when he first introduced me to the members of his pack. That was close to four weeks ago, right after the last full moon—which, I can tell from the gnawing ache pulling at my joints, will be upon us again any day now.

But thinking about Logan's family has me worrying about Malcolm and the others who disappeared outside the master's mansion. I swallow the knot tightening my throat and wonder if they were involved in this bloodbath, or if they're still missing, either caught by the PTF or on the run from deadly, shape shifting panthers in California wine country.

"We can't stay here," Logan says quietly as he moves past my father and me to lead Nova outdoors. The hard lines on his face soften and there is real relief in his eyes when he lowers his voice and adds, "Nova said most of our pack made it out alive. Some might even be at our den just over that peak." He stops to jut his chin toward the eastern mountain. "She has more information but right now she's in no shape to talk. She has to shift and heal herself first."

As I watch them step over the rubble, and make their way through the crumbling house, I get the oddest feeling that something's not quite right here. Heightening my senses, I listen to Nova's blood pulse effortlessly through her veins. As I take in the smooth, unrestricted flow, I quickly conclude that the steady, rhythmic beat of her heart belies her stricken expression. Maybe she's not quite as frightened as she seems.

When Logan disappears around the corner with her packaged in his arms, I think about canine self preservation. While I understand that she's been through a great amount of trauma, I also understand shifting to heal is as inherent as breathing—so why hasn't Nova done it already?

What has her wolf been waiting for?

ABOUT CAT

New York Times and *USA today* Bestselling author, Cathryn Fox/Cat Kalen is a wife, mom, sister, daughter, and friend. She loves dogs, sunny weather, anything chocolate (she never says no to a brownie) pizza and red wine. She has two teenagers who keep her busy with their never ending activities, and a husband who is convinced he can turn her into a mixed martial arts fan. Cathryn can never find balance in her life, is always trying to find time to go to the gym, can never keep up with emails, Facebook or Twitter and tries to write page-turning books that her readers will love.

Connect with Cathryn:
Newsletter
https://app.mailerlite.com/webforms/landing/c1f8n1
Twitter: https://twitter.com/writercatfox
Facebook:
https://www.facebook.com/AuthorCathrynFox?ref=hl
Blog: http://cathrynfox.com/blog/
Goodreads:
https://www.goodreads.com/author/show/91799.Cathryn_Fox

Pinterest http://www.pinterest.com/catkalen/